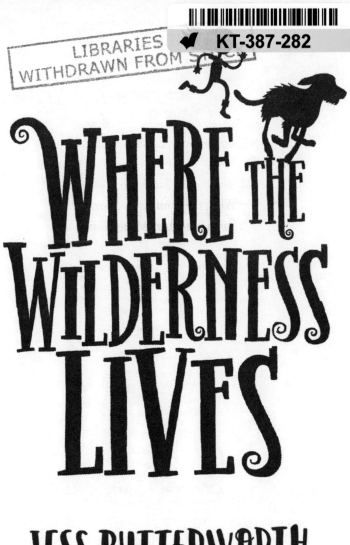

WHERE THE WILDERNESS LIVES

JESS BUTTERWORTH

Orion

ORION CHILDREN'S BOOKS

First published in Great Britain in 2020
by Hodder and Stoughton

1 3 5 7 9 10 8 6 4 2

A CIP catalogue record for this book
is available from the British Library.

ISBN 978 1 51010 550 8

Typeset in Mrs Eaves by Hewer Text UK Ltd, Edinburgh
Printed and bound in Great Britain by Clays Ltd, Elcograf S.p.A.

The paper and board used in this book are made
from wood from responsible sources.

Orion Children's Books
An imprint of
Hachette Children's Group
Part of Hodder and Stoughton
Carmelite House
50 Victoria Embankment
London EC4Y 0DZ

An Hachette UK Company

www.hachette.co.uk
www.hachettechildrens.co.uk

*To anyone who's ever felt
the cry of the wilderness*

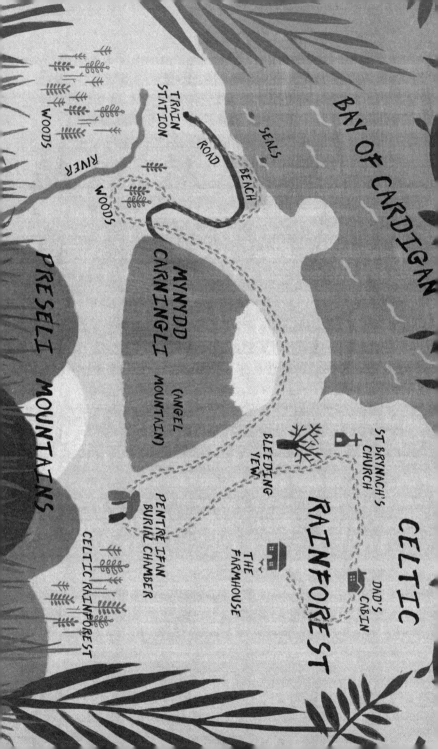

December 16th – Present Day

If I told you that you were going to find a locked safe one day after school, and that it was going to transform your life, you'd probably think either:

1. I'm lying.

Or …

2. That the safe was filled with a huge amount of money.

Well, I'm not lying. I really did find a safe after school. But it wasn't full of money either. Still, it really did change our lives for ever.

But to tell this story properly, I need to start at the beginning …

One and a half thousand years ago there lived a girl who was as strong as an oak tree, as fierce as a holly bush and as wild as ivy. Her name was Gwyon.

Chapter One: Autumn

6 Weeks Earlier

The day we find the safe is a special day. The canal trust has drained a section of the canal for the first time in twenty years, revealing all sorts of treasure stuck under the water.

That morning, we beg Mum to let us stay home from school to search the canal. I do most of the begging; I'll try anything to stop having to go to school right now. My younger brothers and sister, Enzo, Arianwen and Bryn, are lucky. They're still in primary school, together, whereas I have to go to secondary school.

Alone.

But Mum strokes my hair and says, 'No, *mi niña*,' in her Spanish accent. 'Today is a school day.'

Instead, after school, we rush home as fast as we can. When we get back, Mum is standing in the kitchen of the boat wearing an apron over her scrubs. Pasta simmers on the stove and she's chopping a tomato.

'Are you ready?' I ask, worried that all the treasure will be gone by the time we get there. 'Please can we go now?'

'Why don't you join the canal clean-up crew while I finish up dinner,' Mum replies. 'I'll be there soon.'

Every month, people who live along the canal gather to pick up litter scattered on the towpath and in the water, and they've organised today's clean-up to coincide with the drained canal.

4

We see the crew at work, armed with fishing nets and rods, and cycle to meet them. Our Irish wolfhound, Willow, bounds alongside us wearing her burgundy assistant dog harness. It's drizzling, and I pull my hood up. Ahead of me, cycling side by side, Aria and Bryn race each other, speeding through puddles. The flecks of red in Aria's dark curls catch the low winter sun. Even though they're twins, they look nothing alike. Bryn has a blond wavy lion mane of messy hair which he refuses to cut. Aria is taller than he is too. There's a three-year gap between each of us: Aria and Bryn are six, Enzo's nine and I'm twelve.

We join the crew by the aqueduct, between the pub and the crystal shop, under the autumn trees. Tom waves us over.

'Great to have you here to help!' he says.

Tom has a tug boat and I can see that some people are already standing on it to reach the rubbish in the water with nets, scooping up anything floating in the canal. Michael, an older man with a smooth head, is handing out bin liners and dividing people into groups.

Michael's boat is moored next to the aqueduct. Intricate wood carvings decorate the hull like a Viking ship and prayer flags hang on the roof. Mum's best friend, Sam, is here too, with her baby, Ella, held to her chest in a sling. When

Aria and Bryn were little, Mum used to carry them like that. I did too, sometimes.

'Why don't you lot come this way,' Michael says to our group, and we follow him towards the drained part of the canal, pushing our bikes. Excitement bubbles in my stomach; I've lived on the canal since I was six, but I've never seen what it looks like without water in it. We stop to collect rubbish along the way.

Water sounds all around us: Tom's boat engine churns up waves; crisp packets and cans drip as they're lifted from the canal; the current sloshes against the bank.

At last, we reach the section that's been drained. A group of people in yellow high-visibility jackets stand on the edge of the towpath ahead, peering into the canal. We pass a blue working boat loaded with bent shopping trollies, plastic bottles and hundreds of plastic bags, dribbling sludge off the side and into the water.

We lay our bikes on top of each other on the grassy verge and push through the group of people. Everyone always jumps out of the way for Willow. Even though she's the gentlest, most well-trained dog, her size intimidates people.

On the other side of the lock gate, the canal has been completely emptied of water. It's deeper than I expected it to be, about ten feet. At the bottom, covered in brown gloop, is an assortment of tyres, rusty bikes, bits of metal, plastic, fishing rods, traffic cones and lots of other objects I can't distinguish.

'Look at all that stuff!' shouts Bryn. 'I bet some of it's treasure.'

We sit in a line with our legs dangling over the edge and reach down with our nets and poles, trying to hook objects out. Willow lies beside us.

Enzo manages to catch on to something and yanks it out from the sludge, reeling it in.

He laughs as he pulls it closer.

A shoe dangles on the line, dripping slime from its tangled laces. 'I've caught the first treasure!' Enzo says, using sign language.

'Ew,' says Bryn. 'That's not treasure.'

'There's something shiny down there,' says Aria, and she points excitedly towards the middle of the canal.

I squint to try and see what she's aiming at. There's definitely something glistening in the muck.

'Our nets won't reach that far,' says Enzo. 'We've got to get down there.'

A few people are already standing at the bottom amongst the mud in extra-long wellies and gloves, passing the contents back out to the people on the bank.

There's also a ladder built into the canal wall. We don't have much time until Mum gets here and there's no way she'd let us climb into the canal so we'd better get down there.

'Come on, then,' I say. 'Let's check it out.' I sign as I speak. After Enzo was born, Mum and Dad made sure that we were all fluent.

'Those poor fish,' says Aria, shaking her head as we walk towards the ladder. 'There must be hardly any space for them to swim with all that rubbish in there.'

'And the swans, the ducks and the moorhens,' I add.

'I didn't realise it would be so muddy,' says Bryn.

We reach the ladder and Enzo rolls up his trousers and jumper sleeves and climbs down into the muck.

'I'll go first,' he says.

'Don't forget this,' I say, passing him our stick to sift through the mud and junk.

He nods, his eyes sparkling. I realise he's already spotted something good.

Aria and Bryn follow him and I climb down after them, leaving Willow standing on the bank, watching us nervously with pricked-up ears. My feet squelch as I reach the bottom. I'm up to my knees in the mud.

Aria wades toward her mysterious object, bends and pulls out a metal windlass, mostly coated in goop. Windlasses are big, hollow

8

L-shaped keys used to open the lock gates. She sighs. 'I really thought it was going to be an old coin or ancient jewellery.'

Within a few minutes Enzo finds two more windlasses.

'Can I bring this home?' asks Bryn, dragging a rusty bicycle frame behind him. 'Please, please, please?'

'It won't work,' I say to him. 'Look how rusty the pedals are.'

Bryn sticks his bottom lip out. 'I thought we'd get loads of good stuff in here but everything's rubbish.'

Aria wades back towards us and trips. Enzo catches her just before she falls face first into the sludge.

Willow barks, worried from the path above.

'What was that?' asks Aria, peering into the mud behind her with a wrinkled forehead.

Willow whines and paces back and forth, trying to get down to us.

'Time for us to get out,' I say, imagining Aria cutting herself on one of the sharp bits of metal.

'Wait,' says Aria, poking the bottom with her foot. 'I want to see what I slipped on.'

Enzo clears the mud around the object. Aria bends and pulls out a box coated in grime. She wipes away the sludge from one side of it and holds it up to show us.

'I think it's a safe,' I say, noticing the lock on the front. I peer more closely. It's like a safe you'd see in a hotel room — small, about the size of a shoebox, with a handle on the top.

Bryn, who's been sulking, jumps up to get a better look. 'Give it here! Maybe we can open it.'

'Everyone out first,' I say, ushering them back to the wall of the canal. 'Let's pass the safe and the windlasses up the ladder.'

We stand one behind another on different rungs of the ladder and hand the safe up to each other, holding on to the ladder with one hand and grabbing the handle with the other.

'You children shouldn't be playing in there,' says a passer-by.

I ignore him and pass the safe to Bryn.

Bryn's on the top rung, covered in green and brown slime. 'It's heavy,' he says as he drops it on the ground. He takes the windlasses from me one by one and places them on the path, before clambering over the edge of the canal wall. Willow barks and licks his face.

The rest of us follow him up.

Crowding around the metal box, we examine it. Willow lies down next to us, wagging her tail as people pass.

'Look!' I say, staring at the circular dial with the numbers one to ten written around the outside, scratched and rusty but still legible. 'It has a dial combination lock. You spin the arrow on the dial to match whatever the code is.'

'I wonder what's inside,' says Aria. 'I bet it's money.'

I spot Mum in her blue work scrubs, searching for us through the crowd. Her eyes grow wide as she sees us, covered in mud, and I know she's going to say I should have known better than to let my brothers and sister climb into the canal. But it was worth it. Because now we have a safe that's full of money and is going to change our lives. Maybe I'll never have to go to school again.

If only we can get it open.

As a child, Gwyon felt the pulse of the Earth under her bare feet and the rush of life in the trees. Every day she would explore the forest, and arrive home covered in mud, or followed by a new animal, often a fox, hedgehog or blackbird. The only thing Gwyon cared about as much as the forest and the animals was her brother.

Chapter Two
Canal

I watch Mum pause to say hi and chat to our neighbours, Jenny and Raj, while Bryn and Aria continue to discuss the safe.

'Money would be boring,' Bryn says to Aria. 'And wouldn't it be all wet and rotten by now?'

I wonder if the safe's waterproof.

'It's pretty rusty,' says Enzo. 'I bet we can get it open.'

Bryn grins and lifts the safe on to his lap. 'I knew we'd find real treasure. Can I try and open it?' he asks, rattling the lock.

One of the organisers passes us and frowns. 'You're not supposed to take the things you pick up.'

'But it's all getting thrown away anyway, right?' replies Bryn.

'Yes, but it might be dangerous,' she says. 'There's no way to know what might be inside.'

This only fuels Bryn's and Aria's imaginations even more.

'Maybe it's an ancient scarab beetle,' says Bryn.

'Or a mummy,' says Aria.

'You can't fit a mummy in there,' says Enzo. They've been learning about ancient Egypt at school.

'You could if it was a mummified cat,' replies Aria, crossing her arms.

'Or a mummified hamster!' says Bryn.

'Here's Mum!' I shout, as she approaches us, pushing her bike.

14

'How about this: if your mum says you can keep it then it's fine,' suggests the organiser.

'What on earth happened here?' asks Mum. She tuts at our muddy legs.

'We found a safe,' says Bryn, tugging at her arm. 'Can we keep it?'

'It's covered in dirt,' she says. 'Do you really want it?'

'We'll clean it,' says Aria, giving Mum her best smile.

'Then I don't see why not,' says Mum. 'It could be exciting.'

'Yes!' says Bryn, punching the air above him.

Just then a news crew arrives and the organiser goes over to welcome them.

We stand back and examine our treasure.

One locked safe.

Three windlasses.

And an old shoe.

I watch as the local news team films the drained canal and chats to the organiser.

Then the interviewer, a lady with short blonde hair and pink lipstick, approaches us.

'Hello, kids. Were you excited to see the canal emptied?'

We all nod eagerly and she smiles.

'Do you mind if we interview you for the local news?'

'If they want to be?' says Mum, looking at us.

I say that I want to, with the others. But when the two cameras point at us, I suddenly feel self-conscious. Usually I'd take every opportunity to talk about the canal and how proud I am to live on it, but now all I can think of is the people from school who might watch this. I wonder what they'll think of me standing here, covered in mud and rubbish.

I've been at my new school for almost two months but still the only person I'm friends with is Jasmine and that's because we went to primary school together. And we only have English lessons together so I don't see her that much. Yesterday and today I couldn't find her at lunch and I had to eat by myself in the cafeteria.

It's not like I haven't tried to make friends. It's just that everyone already knows each other and I'm not sure where I fit in.

Thankfully Aria immediately points to our pile of treasure, starting with the shoe, and I don't have to say anything.

Maybe people won't even notice me.

Enzo models the windlasses, holding them at either side of his body.

'What was the most exciting thing you found in the drained canal today?' asks the interviewer.

'This safe!' answers Bryn. 'It's really scratched up and it's locked. But maybe there's a diamond ring inside.'

'Well, keep us updated if you get it open! I'm sure the viewers would love to see what's inside too.'

'We'll get it open,' says Aria. 'Mum says we can teach ourselves to do anything if we work at it.'

The interviewer smiles at us. 'Very best of luck with that.' She turns to the camera and talks into it as she walks off, wrapping up the news segment.

'How many numbers do you think the combination is?' asks Enzo.

'I bet it's six numbers,' I say. I've used a combination lock once before, for my locker at gym, and it was six numbers. 'But I guess it could also be a different kind.'

Enzo thinks for a second. His green eyes focus on the path.

'If it's six, that means there are a million different combinations,' he says.

'A million!' says Bryn, eyes wide with disbelief. 'How long will it take to try all of those?'

Enzo squeezes his eyes shut as he thinks.

'How long does it take to count to a million?' he says. 'Let's say you can do one combination every second. That's one million seconds, which is about . . . 278 hours, which is about . . . eleven or twelve days, if we work nonstop.'

'That's for ever!' says Aria, stamping her foot.

Mum laughs. 'I'm sure you'll find a way. Quick maths, Enzo.'

Bryn twists the combination dial on the safe. It squeaks and sticks but the numbers eventually turn. Bryn yanks the door. It doesn't budge.

'Let's get you home and cleaned up before dark,' says Mum.

We strap the safe on to the bike trailer Mum has brought with her. The twins used to ride in it when they were younger. Now we use the trailer to bring the fuel, shopping and wood along the canal to the boat. You can't reach us by car.

Next, we slowly ride home together, stopping to pick up any litter that's still on the ground.

'Look at all this rubbish,' says Mum, holding up a crisp packet and a cotton bud stick.

'At least we're getting rid of it,' says Aria, reaching for Mum's hand to make her feel better.

'We're just moving it to a landfill,' says Mum, shaking her head. 'Almost all of the plastic ever created still exists somewhere in the world today.'

I smile sympathetically at Aria. There isn't much we can say to cheer Mum up when it comes to things like this. We already know how much plastic frustrates her. The first time Mum tore the plastic wrapping off the vegetables at the supermarket checkout I was mortified. She held up the queue behind us for ages.

Later, after she'd calmed down, she explained that most plastic can only be used once, and after it's thrown away it adds to the tons of plastic waste that already exists. It covers the land, floats in the sea and leaks into our drinking water, for thousands of years.

After that, every time we went shopping, I did it too.

Until I started at the new school.

What if someone from my year saw me? What would they think?

Out of the corner of my eye, I spot a heron on the other side of the bank, poised and still, watching for fish.

Willow bounds ahead, splashing in the puddles and the heron jolts at the noise, spreads its huge wings and flies off. The orange setting sun reflects in the ripples of the water.

As we cycle along, I remember how back in spring the hedgerow verges were covered in buttercups, blossom and cowslip. Now they look totally different, bursting with tufts of Old Man's Beard, bright berries and prickly brambles. It's the time of year where people start to light their wood-burners and smoke billows up from the chimneys on the boats. We pass a slightly sunken carved pumpkin sitting on the roof of one of the boats, left over from Halloween last week.

I breathe in the cool air and taste the wood smoke, happy that it's Friday and I don't have to go back to school for two whole days.

One day, Gwyon's brother developed a high fever. Gwyon tried everything she could to make him better. Gwyon knew a lot about the plants in the forest, but she didn't know how to mix them into healing potions. And she was sure that there was a potion that would save him. She just had to find someone who knew how to make it.

Chapter Three
Newt

On the way home, we pass lots of different moored boats, some with pristine shiny paintwork and names like *Serene* or *Kingfisher*, others with chipped paint and piles of stuff on the roofs buried under tarps. We pass *Narrow Escape*, *Mudlark*, *Puddleduck* and *The Unsinkable II*.

In summer, we move up and down the canal but in winter we have a permanent mooring and stay mainly in one spot, between the town and the village. It's still remote but closer to drinking water and a place to empty the toilet tank and things like that. There isn't enough daylight in winter to move the boat after Mum gets home from work. At this time of year there's lots of space between the boats, whereas in summer we always have someone moored right next to us.

After about ten minutes, our boat, *Newt*, comes into view. A wood and glass cockpit encloses the very back of the boat, where the tiller and our main entrance is. Her name is written in dark-green and black lettering on the side. Solar panels cover one third of the roof. The outer edges are lined with plant pots, benches that we made from wooden crates, and bags of solid fuel for the burner. Sometimes people ask if I wish I had a garden but I know that the whole countryside is my garden.

We hose Willow down on the towpath and dry

her off with towels, each rubbing a leg. She stands patiently, waiting, sometimes licking Aria's hair with her long tongue. Next, we clean the safe. Under the mud it's covered in a dark-red rust that flakes off under my fingertips.

Inside, our boat's layout goes like this: cockpit, entrance, galley kitchen, table, sitting room, bathroom at the side, then all the bedrooms at the back. My bedroom is more of a nook than a room, but I like it because it's cosy. Photographs of Mum and Dad and my siblings cover the walls, and curtains separate it from the rest of the boat.

There are all sorts of special modifications that we have to make living on a boat easier. We have a tiny television that fits inside a cupboard when we're not using it, although most of the time the signal is pretty terrible. The twins have bunk beds to save space. One of the coolest things is that the kitchen cooker is on gimbals which allow the cooker to swing, so even if the boat rocks, the saucepan stays upright and won't spill.

At the moment, the kitchen shelves are filled with homemade rosehip and blackberry-and-apple jams and hazelnut butter. This is my favourite time of year because we get to forage for the food that grows in the hedgerows along the towpath. Every time I walk Willow I take a bowl for picking berries, always making sure I leave lots for the animals to eat too.

I step into the bathroom. On the windowsill is a big glass jar. I've been trying to grow a velvety blanket of wood moss in it. Aria wants to turn it into a fairy garden when I'm finished. So far, there's only a tiny patch on a rock but I'm confident it will grow eventually.

My stomach rumbles and I remember that I hardly ate lunch today. I hated sitting by myself so much I wasn't hungry.

I wonder where Jasmine was?

After I've changed out of my wet clothes, I text Jasmine and ask if she wants to sleepover tomorrow after Bonfire Night. Last year we went together and then she came back to the boat. We hid under the covers with hot chocolate and told ghost stories until Mum came in to tell us to be quiet and we were both so scared we screamed.

A few minutes later, a reply flashes on my screen.

Sorry, going with my dad this year.

I sigh.

'Cara!' shouts Bryn. 'Come quickly! The canal is on the telly!'

I slide off the bed and run out to the living room.

Everyone is gathered around the television,

clustered on rugs, floor cushions and leather poufs. Aria's sitting closest to the telly, almost right in front of it, and Mum asks her to move back, patting the cushion beside her. I pull on my thick woolly socks and join them, sitting between Willow and Enzo and stroking Willow's soft fur. Next to Enzo, Bryn grips the safe on his lap.

It's the evening news. The camera pans along the canal, lingering on the dripping shopping trolleys being pulled out of the water. The newsreader we met today is talking.

'After a boat got stuck on the debris sitting in the bottom of the canal, the trust decided to drain the canal for the first time in twenty years to remove the rubbish,' says the interviewer on TV, as she strolls along the towpath.

'I talked to some local children about what they were able to remove from the canal,' the reporter continues.

Our faces appear on the TV and everyone squeals and whoops.

'Look! We're famous!' says Aria, and she pouts and walks up and down posing. 'I always knew I'd be famous.'

'I'm *trying* to listen,' says Bryn.

'These are windlasses,' Aria is saying on the screen. 'They're very useful for opening the locks.'

'But most of the stuff in the canal is rubbish,'

says Bryn. 'Like this shoe!'

I'm relieved that with Aria and Bryn explaining, and Enzo displaying the findings, you hardly notice I'm there, standing quietly behind them.

The interviewer turns back to the camera and we disappear from the shot. 'What a pleasure to see the community here come together to clean up this area,' she says. 'Together, they will work to make it a safer place for wildlife, fish, boaters and people enjoying the beauty of the canal.'

She smiles, and then the news moves on to the next thing.

After dinner Enzo stacks logs in the wood burner and sparks fly up the flue pipe to the chimney.

'It'll be nice and warm soon,' he says.

We have a metal fan that sits on top of the burner and spins when the heat rises, circulating the hot air around the whole boat.

The fire roars and soon it's toasty inside. Mum reads a story aloud, curled up on the sofa with Aria and Bryn. She's finally convinced Bryn to put down the safe. Her singsong voice crescendos as she reaches the end of a chapter.

Tomorrow I'll try and find a way to open the

safe. You never know, I might get lucky and guess the code straight away.

I sit cross-legged on the rug opposite from Enzo, playing backgammon and listening. Outside, a fox barks.

I smile. Autumn evenings are my favourite. The only thing that could make this better is if Dad was here too.

Gwyon was determined to find a potion to heal her brother. Her mother told Gwyon that she had less than a year to find a cure. After that, it would be too late. Gwyon asked everyone she knew for help, and eventually someone told her of a sorceress who could perhaps help her — and so Gwyon set off to find her.

Chapter Four

Bonfire

The next day is the fifth of November. Bonfire Night. That evening, I braid my hair into two French plaits either side of my head, before pulling my woolly hat on.

'I promise I'll be warm enough,' says Bryn from the living area, arguing with Mum.

'You don't have enough layers, *mi amor*,' says Mum. 'You need to wear your raincoat over the top of it.'

I step outside my bedroom. Bryn is insisting on wearing his Halloween costume to the bonfire evening and is jumping up and down in his green dinosaur onesie.

'But I don't want to wear my raincoat,' says Bryn. 'Dinosaurs don't wear raincoats. And it's not even raining.'

'Here,' says Enzo, bringing out one of his stripy jumpers. 'Dinosaurs love wearing stripes.'

'They do?' asks Bryn.

Enzo nods and does a dinosaur impression that also looks a bit like a chicken.

'Thanks!' says Bryn, grinning. He slips the jumper over his head. The material swamps him but the dinosaur tail sticks out of the bottom and the teeth and eyes on the hood poke out of the top.

'That will do,' says Mum, slipping his raincoat into a backpack.

Bryn stomps around the boat, imitating a tyrannosaurus. He's one of those kids that's always on the move, always dancing, tapping his feet under the table or bopping his head. He can't concentrate unless he's moving.

This is the one night of the year where we don't bring Willow with us. As a hearing dog, she's been specially trained to cope with loud noises and busy places, but we brought her with us a few years ago and Enzo noticed she didn't wag her tail once. He decided that she must have been scared.

I pat her head as I leave and whisper, 'We'll be back soon.'

We arrive at the bonfire as the sun sets. The event is held in a large field and birds twitter above our heads, flying in and out of the hedgerows. About two hundred people are milling around, some gathered around a truck selling toffee apples and warm drinks, which is parked next to a local folk band playing the guitar and violin. An excited chatter fills the air.

'What are they doing?' asks Aria, pointing to group of people in fluorescent jackets around the huge unlit bonfire, which is fenced off in the corner of the field. They're shining torches on the pile, and prodding it with long sticks.

'They're searching for hedgehogs, darling,' says Mum. 'Sometimes they crawl inside while the fire is being built and then they're stuck once it's lit.'

Aria turns and looks up at her, horrified.

'Don't worry,' says Mum. 'That's why they're checking for them now. They'll remove them all before they light the fire.'

As it gets dark, the crowd becomes a sea of hats. The cold bites and I slip my gloves on.

'Remember, remember, the fifth of November,' the twins chant together.

People light sparklers and dazzling swirls of light cut through the darkness, leaving the smell of matches and charcoal behind.

We join the queue for toffee apples. The smell of winter spices, cinnamon and cloves, fills the air.

'Do you think they have hot chocolate?' asks a person behind me. I recognise her voice and turn around. It's Aisha from my English class. Her short black hair sticks out under a furry headband and her silver hoop earrings catch the light. She's there with Sophie, Keaton and Mo. Keaton's the tallest of the group by a whole foot and is bundled up in a bright-blue puffer jacket. Dark freckles cover his nose and cheekbones.

I smile and say, 'Hey!'

Then I notice someone else with them too.

It's Jasmine.

I look behind her for her dad but he's nowhere to be seen. There aren't any adults with them at all. And no younger brothers or sisters either.

'I thought your dad was coming,' I say.

'He changed his mind at the last minute,' she says, but she stares at the ground and I know she's lying.

The others are already chatting amongst themselves.

Why didn't she invite me?

I'm wearing too many layers and underneath them my skin is hot and sweaty.

Jasmine turns away from me and towards her new friends, paying more attention than is necessary to Keaton's story about how he's never been to the fireworks display before.

'Aria needs the toilet' says Mum.

'I'll take her,' I say quickly, desperate to be anywhere but here. 'You get the drinks.'

I grip Aria's hand as we wind through the crowd to the toilets.

My skin crawls as I think about what's happening back in the queue. I wonder if they've seen Bryn's weird outfit and are laughing at him.

Did Jasmine tell them I wanted to come tonight, and they told her not to invite me?

Or did she not mention me at all?

Aria disappears inside the cubicle and I wrap my arms around myself while I wait for her, feeling sick to my stomach.

'Can we go to the sparklers now?' asks Aria, once she emerges.

'No,' I snap at her.

She scowls at me.

It's not her fault, I remind myself.

'I'm sorry,' I say, softening my voice. 'Maybe in a minute. We have to wait for Mum here.'

After a few minutes, Mum, Enzo and Bryn hurry over, balancing paper cups of hot apple juice in their hands.

'They're about to light the fire,' says Bryn, passing me a cup.

Aria takes hers from Enzo and drinks it quickly, smacking her lips. She hands Mum her empty cup, takes Bryn's hand and they skip ahead to the fire.

We're just in time to see the fire take hold. The flames lick and curl, enclosing the wood and giving off heat, though it doesn't stop a cold lump creeping into the back of my throat. I bite back tears. Jasmine was all I had at school. And now I don't even have her.

'Fireworks! It's time for fireworks!' shrieks Aria.

The first one explodes into the night sky like a rocket, showering us with gold. The crowd oohs and ahhs.

34

Bryn holds my hand and smiles at me. I try to smile back.

'I love those ones,' shouts Aria, pointing at a stream of green light curling through the sky.

'Me too,' I say.

Across the other side of the fire, illuminated by the flames, I spot Jasmine and the others, laughing and joking together. Jasmine has her arm linked through Sophie's.

My heart fills with sadness watching them.

I shake my head and pull my eyes away, back up towards the glittering lights.

After two months of searching, Gwyon found the sorceress, who agreed to teach Gwyon how to make the potion she needed. In exchange, Gwyon would have to work as the sorceress's apprentice. Willing to do anything to save her brother, Gwyon agreed.

Chapter Five

Badger

I wake up to rain hammering on the roof. Condensation has gathered on the inside of the window next to my bed.

I shiver and pull the duvet over my head. Sunday is chore day, or 'hands-on living day' as Mum calls it. If we don't do everything on the checklist then we won't have drinking water, clean clothes or wood for the burner.

Sunday also means I have to go to school tomorrow. I sigh. I wish I could just stay in bed all day.

Willow pushes her nose through the curtain and rests her head on my bed. I stroke her wiry hair.

'You get it, don't you?' I say to her, wishing I could be Willow for a day.

She groans in response and closes her eyes.

I hear the diesel boat pull up and begin to refill *Newt*'s engine tank.

'Breakfast's ready!' shouts Mum from the kitchen.

I reluctantly sit up, throw my legs over the side of the bed and stand up. Wrapping my dressing gown over my pyjamas, I leave my nook and step along the corridor to the living area.

Bryn is sitting on the floor and trying to prise the safe open with a butter knife. 'Mum?' he says. 'Can we take this to someone to open it?'

'I'm not sure I know anyone who'd be able to

open a locked safe,' replies Mum, as she flips a pancake over the hob.

'You must know someone,' says Bryn.

I can tell it's driving Bryn crazy not being able to open it. A part of me is desperate to find out what's inside too but right now it doesn't seem as important as figuring out how I'm going to get through the next week of school.

'I'll have a think about it,' says Mum.

Bryn continues to stab at the hinge of the safe with the knife. 'It's not fair. It won't budge.'

'I think that's the point,' says Enzo.

Mum laughs.

'It's time to call Dad!' shouts Aria, pointing at the clock.

It's nine o'clock. We always chat on a Sunday at this time. Dad lives in Wales. He met Mum in London when she came over from Spain to study at university there. We all lived on *Newt* together until three years ago, when they separated. A few months later, Dad was given a grant to study rare plants in Wales. We go and visit him but it's not the same. The last time I saw him was right before my birthday a few weeks ago. We planted an apple sapling together.

'In twelve years this little tree will be grown up — just like you,' Dad had said.

We prop Mum's phone up against the window in the living room, the only place where the signal's strong enough to video chat, and gather in front of it. His face pops up on the screen and he smiles as he sees us. 'Hi, everyone!'

We tell him about the canal clean-up and finding the safe, and then Bonfire Night.

'That sounds like fun!' he replies. 'What are you planning to do with a locked safe?'

'We're going to try and get it open,' says Bryn. 'Mum's going to see if she can think of anyone who could help.'

'What have you been up to, Dad?' asks Enzo.

'Well, tomorrow I'm going on a research trip to a remote forest near Snowdonia called Coed Felinrhyd to study blackberries in custard,' Dad says. His voice always gets higher when he's excited about something.

'What's blackberries in custard?' Enzo says, signing in front of the screen.

'That rare lichen I showed you once,' replies Dad. 'It has clusters of black dots on a yellow or green background and grows on the trunks of hazel trees.'

Enzo nods.

'When are you back?' asks Aria.

'I'll be back at my cabin on Thursday night,' says Dad. 'And this weekend I'll come and visit you. I can't wait!'

Usually I love talking to Dad but not today. Today I just want to be alone. I wave goodbye to him while the twins are chattering away about a school project and sit at the table next to the pile of pancakes.

'You're quiet today, *mi niña*,' Mum says, rubbing my back. 'Is everything OK?'

I nod but don't look at her. She'll know something's wrong if I meet her eyes.

'Breakfast's done. Water tank's filled. I'm going to shower,' says Mum, and she hums as she walks down the corridor.

Two minutes later there's a shriek from the bathroom.

'Did someone put *bubble bath* in the toilet?' shouts Mum. Her voice is tight.

Aria and Bryn raise their eyebrows at each other.

'We've got to go, Dad. Bye! Love you!' says Aria.

We all gather outside the bathroom. A sea of bubbles cover the tiles on the floor, glistening with rainbows and popping.

'I'm sorry, Mum,' says Bryn. 'We wanted to clean the toilet for you.'

'We were trying to be helpful,' says Aria.

Mum takes a deep breath and her tense expression softens.

'I appreciate the thought,' Mum says, soaking up the bubbles with a towel. 'But never again, please. That's a job for me. Why don't you all take Willow for a walk while I clean this up? It's finally stopped raining.'

'Come on,' I say to everyone. 'Let's finish breakfast then go.'

Mum smiles a thank you at me. 'And then I can finally have that shower,' she says. '*Without* bubbles.'

Outside on the deck, I see a woman in a beige raincoat walking along the path. She slows as she approaches our boat and I notice her eyes narrow and an expression crosses her face that I've seen before.

Ignore her, I think.

'I'll get the bikes down,' I say to the others.

I unlock them from the roof of *Newt* and pass them in assembly-line style, one by one, to Enzo, who hands them down the plank to Bryn, where Aria is waiting on the towpath. Bryn wobbles on the plank and the woman tuts and shakes her head.

'Ready!' says Aria. She props the last bike up next to her.

The lady eyes the twins' outfits. Today Aria is wearing several of Mum's scarves wrapped around her neck and a superhero cape is billowing behind her. Bryn's wearing an oversized raincoat and sparkling purple wellies.

I leap from the roof of the boat down on to the towpath in my wellies. My feet squelch in the mud. We mount the bikes.

The woman purses her lips and murmurs something under her breath, a disapproving frown forming on her face.

'Hi,' I say to her as I put my foot on the bike pedal.

'Do you children have a toilet on there?' she asks.

I can't help myself.

'It's right there,' I say, pointing at the ground beneath her. 'You're standing on it.'

Her eyes shoot to the mud at her feet, eyes wide and horrified, and she speeds away.

'That's mean,' whispers Aria, tugging my sleeve. 'Maybe she wanted to use it.'

'I doubt it,' I reply.

'Maybe she was really desperate,' she says, staring up at me with her big dark eyes.

I sigh, turn around, and using my most polite voice I shout after the woman, 'Would you like to use the facilities?'

'We do have a real loo!' adds Aria.

'And a washing machine,' says Bryn brightly.

'No, I would not,' the woman says, marching down the towpath away from us.

'It was obviously a joke,' says Enzo. 'We wouldn't poo outside.'

'Exactly,' says Bryn. 'And if we did have to poo outside we'd dig a hole, far away from any water source. She must know that.'

I shrug it off, but a new worry creeps into my mind.

What if everyone at school feels the same way about living on a boat as that woman?

I call Willow but she doesn't come. She could win a prize for being the biggest dog but also one for being the laziest.

'Willow!' I shout again. After a minute, the boat rocks as she bounds out of the hatch, leaps off the front of the deck and lands in the mud. Her ears are pricked and her tail wags back and forth at full speed. She nuzzles her head into my side, able to tell that I'm feeling bad. It makes me smile for a second.

Mum taps on the window from inside. She's saying something. I can't hear her through the glass.

'She says that we should be back for lunch,' says Enzo.

'Thanks,' I say, and give Mum a thumbs-up. Enzo's ability to read Mum's and our lips sometimes feels like having a brother with a superpower.

'Let's go!' I say, kicking off and cycling along the path.

We have a busy morning combing the hedgerows for berries, cycling along the canal, and then, after lunch, curling up in front of the fire and trying to crack the safe.

That evening, after dinner, we take our cooked vegetable leftovers outside and empty them out in the hedgerow at the side of the towpath. Enzo adds a dollop of peanut butter to the mix.

'For our special visitors,' he says.

Back inside, we sit at the window facing the towpath and wait.

After ten minutes, Aria groans loudly. 'How long is this going to take?' she asks.

'Just wait a few more minutes,' I say.

And then we see one.

A black-and-white striped badger bumbles up to the food, puts his snout in it and eats.

We'd spotted a badger sett nearby on our walk earlier and Mum had suggested putting out some food to see if we could tempt the badgers out.

'Look!' says Aria, pointing as another badger joins the first. 'It's a whole family.'

'They're called clans,' I say. 'Now remember, you can't tell anyone about this. Some people kill badgers because they think they might transmit disease to cows.'

Everyone nods and Bryn pretends to zip up his lips.

When I was younger we'd often see badgers outside. Now these are the first ones I've seen all year.

'I'm going to discover a vaccine against the disease so no more badgers have to die,' says Enzo.

'Sounds like a plan,' I reply.

After about ten minutes, the badgers disappear and I sigh. Now there's no distraction from the thought of school tomorrow.

'What's the matter?' asks Enzo.

I still don't want to talk about what happened at the bonfire. I usually have to sit with my feelings for a while before I'm ready to talk about them. Mum calls me an internal processor. I'm often thinking or daydreaming.

Not like Jasmine. She always says what she's thinking right away. At least, that's what I thought.

But Enzo can read me and my body language. He can tell immediately if there's something bothering me. When he was a baby, Mum told me that he might never be able to hear with his ears. I remember feeling worried that I wouldn't be able to talk to him, but we talk all the time.

'I haven't done my English homework,' I say,

46

which is true. It's just not the whole story.

'What is it?' he asks.

'I have to give a sixty-second presentation on one of my favourite things,' I reply.

'You could talk about us,' says Aria, and I nudge her.

'Or dinosaurs,' adds Bryn.

I laugh.

'What about *Newt*?' asks Enzo. 'I could talk about her for hours.'

'That's actually a good idea,' I reply. That way I'll get my chance to tell everyone what living on *Newt* is really like. That people like the woman in the coat are wrong — it's not dirty and shoddy. It's wonderful.

That night I fall asleep rehearsing the words in my head and trying to ignore the gnawing feeling in my stomach.

December 16th - Present Day

We hadn't forgotten about the safe, of course.
Earlier that evening we tried three things:

1. Prising it open with a knife.
2. Guessing different codes.
3. Hitting it with a hammer.

But it turns out that breaking into a safety deposit box isn't as easy as we thought. Even if it's an old rusty one.

Gwyon had been longing to learn the mysterious ways of the forest since she was a child. Now, finally, she'd have the chance. She could learn from a sorceress and be able to save her brother. And so, she set to work.

Chapter Six
School

The next morning, I grip my bike's handlebars tightly as I pedal along the towpath. The cold seeps in through my gloves to my fingers. It's a clear autumnal day and the sky is bright blue. Leaves crunch beneath the turning tyres and get caught in the spokes. I'm late again.

My thighs burn as I push faster. The brown, green and orange colour of the trees fly past me. The early morning golden sun reflects off the water of the canal and in the windows of the moored narrowboats. Tom waves at me from his deck as I pass.

'Morning!' I shout, not daring to take my hand off the handlebars to wave. The path gets bumpy here.

The towpath is quiet this early. I pass a jogger in green leggings and a few dog walkers but otherwise it's empty. My breath is puffs of condensation.

I reach the aqueduct where the canal is carried over the River Avon. It looks out over rolling fields of sheep and cows. Instead of going over the river, I turn sharply and follow the road underneath it. When I started at this new school, Mum asked me if I wanted to get the bus there like the other kids, but I love cycling, even if the next part of the journey involves a hill. This is the only good part of my day at the minute.

After the hill, I cut up through the woods. A part of me thinks about not going at all. I could happily stay in the woods all day. But I don't want to give up.

What would Mum and Dad think?

I pop out from the trees into the village, cycle along the country road, and there ahead of me is the boxy school building with a sea of red jumpers in front of it. Butterflies gather in my stomach.

I remove my helmet and hang it over my bike, which I lock on the rack.

The final bell rings and I'm grateful that I've timed it just right to not have to stand in the yard with everyone.

In English, I slide into my seat next to Jasmine, careful not to make any eye contact. On the other side of her sits Aisha, staring at her phone under the desk, and Sophie, plaiting a small section of her long glossy hair. In the row behind are Keaton and next to him is Mo, who's moving his lips, practising his talk silently. My heart pounds as I watch Rani give a presentation about football and Oliver talk about his pet dog.

Ms Pepper leaps up from her chair between each presentation and claps enthusiastically. I'm so nervous that none of Ms Pepper's words register until she calls my name to the front. I'm next.

'Cara,' she says with a smile, welcoming me to

the front of the class.

I grip my notes and stand, my chair scraping against the floor. I walk up to the front and turn to face the class. My breath quickens.

'Hi, everyone,' I say. 'My favourite thing that I'm going to talk about today is *Newt*.'

'Like the amphibian?' asks Oliver.

'No interruptions, please,' says Ms Pepper.

My face grows hot.

'No, not like the amphibian. *Newt* is a boat.' I stare down at my notes and read on. '*Newt* is my home. She's like a giant green floating apartment. She has electricity and a bathroom just like any normal house, but if you don't like your neighbours, you can just move. Although we don't have an actual garden, I grow flowers and vegetables on the roof. I get to see all kinds of wildlife, like swans and cygnets, ducks and water voles. Once, when the canal froze, I saw a fox on the ice. We have solar panels for energy.'

Someone sniggers. I can't tell who it is. Maybe Keaton, I think.

I falter. Prickly heat creeps up the back of my neck. The teacher shushes the class.

I glance up. Jasmine is whispering something to Aisha, who nods.

Why don't they want to hang out with me?

I look around at the rest of the class. Mo is sprawled over his desk, head down. Rani's eyes are closed. Everyone else is staring right at me. My mouth dries and I swallow.

Why didn't Jasmine invite me to Bonfire Night with them?

My eyes sting with tears so I bow my head and keep them glued to my piece of paper.

'We have a tank for water and toilet waste that gets emptied every week.' Somehow, the words keep flowing out of my mouth. I hear them get quicker and quicker as I'm desperate to reach the end.

Why did Jasmine lie?

I read the last sentence and hastily walk back to my chair and sit back down. My chair squeaks.

Ms Pepper claps. 'Thank you, Cara! That was brilliant.'

I try and smile but anxiety lands in my stomach.

I can't believe I mentioned the toilet tank.

I replay the words that left my mouth during my speech. It's too late to take them back.

Emily is next but she can't find her notes and the whole class erupts into chatter as we wait.

Aisha leans over Jasmine, who hasn't looked at me once, to talk to me. My heart quickens and I immediately think about all the mean things she might say to me.

'My cousin lives on a narrowboat in London,' she says, smiling. She has a gap between her two front teeth. 'I love it. Can I come and see *Newt* one day?'

'Er, yeah,' I say, taken aback. 'Definitely.'

'I want to see *Newt* too,' Sophie exclaims from Aisha's other side. Jasmine still doesn't say anything. She just looks straight ahead.

'Why don't you give us your number and maybe we can come over some day after school?' Aisha suggests, flipping to the back of her notebook, pen raised.

I tell her my number and she smiles. 'I'll text you.'

I think I hear Jasmine make a sort of scoffing noise under her breath, but at that moment Ms Pepper shushes everyone as Emily walks to the front of the class.

I try and listen to the other presentations but I can't focus. There are too many thoughts flashing through my mind.

Maybe Aisha and Sophie want to be friends. After all, they seemed keen to see Newt.

But what about Jasmine?

After school, I cycle home and for the first time in weeks I don't feel deflated like a flat tyre. Even if Jasmine doesn't want to be my friend any more, at least Aisha and Sophie are talking to me.

I stop at the aqueduct to watch the ducks and check my phone. There's a new text. I open it, wondering if it's from Aisha.

It's from a number I don't recognise.

Now I know why you stink. Boaty.

I freeze, gazing into the canal with its brown water. For a moment I can't even seem to breathe. Blood pounds through my ears. Then my throat opens and suddenly my breath bursts in and out.

I type back.

Who is this?

The canal doesn't stink. I know that much. I turn my head and sniff my arm. I don't think I smell either.

Who is it? How did they get my number?

I wait for a text back.

But there's no reply.

Gwyon began to work for the sorceress. She had to live in the sorceress's house, far away from her mother and brother. Gwyon's room was a cave outside the house where the sorceress mixed her potions above a fire. Gwyon slept on a bed of moss, next to the pots and cauldrons. But, although weeks passed, the sorceress didn't let her make anything. Not one potion. The only tasks Gwyon was allowed to do was stir the pot and stoke the fire with wood.

Chapter Seven
Dad

I stand there for an age. The sun is low by the time I decide to finish cycling home. Orange and purple light streaks across the sky. I switch on my front and back bike lights. It will be dark under the cover of trees further down the towpath. I cycle slowly, not wanting to be home quite yet.

Only a few people at school have my number: Jasmine and Aisha. And Sophie might have written it down when I told it to Aisha this afternoon.

It's not Jasmine's number, I know that. Could it be one of the others? Maybe Aisha and Sophie were just pretending to want to come and see *Newt* but they really wanted my number to send that message?

Wind rustles the branches around me and sends fresh leaves tumbling to the ground. I glance over my shoulder, feeling like I'm being watched, but there's no one there.

I realise that anyone in the row behind me could have heard me say my phone number too.

Reaching *Newt*, I slow down. I spot Mum in the window watering the crocus bulbs she planted. Mum's favourite flowers. At one point, she even wanted to paint *Newt* purple and rename her *Crocus* but we all objected. We love *Newt* and her bright-green colour.

At least, I used to love *Newt*.

Aria and Bryn sit side by side on the roof of the boat, dangling their legs off the side, each holding a fishing net.

'Look what I caught!' says Aria as I stop my bike. She lifts up a pike fish by the tail from the bucket beside her and dangles it in the air.

'I caught a gudgeon,' says Bryn. 'Look, you can tell by its huge head.'

'Well done, you two,' I say. 'But remember what Mum said. You have to let them go before you come inside. No keeping them in buckets.'

'I only wanted to watch it for a while,' says Bryn.

'I know,' I say.

Last time they'd decided to catch fish, they'd left a bucketful of them on the deck. Mum had been hanging the washing out on the line on the roof and stepped in it. Fish went everywhere.

I push my bike up the plank and lock it to everyone else's on the front deck.

'Hi,' I say, pushing open the door and stepping inside.

Enzo is reading a book on his stomach in the centre of the living room, next to Willow. I can just see his nose under his wild dark curls. Willow barks hi at me and Enzo raises his head and waves before returning to his book. Willow bounds towards me. I kneel and squeeze her while she gives me sloppy kisses. She smells of forest honey.

Somehow, Willow always knows when I need extra attention. I pat her head and stroke her shaggy eyebrows and the long wiry hair under her jaw.

'Hi, darling.' Mum looks up from the stove. 'How was school?'

'Fine,' I say, and swing my backpack down.

It was awful.

'Is it getting any easier?'

'A bit,' I say.

It's getting worse.

I try to steer my thoughts away from the phone in my pocket, but it's like I can feel it getting heavier and heavier, weighing me down.

'You know, I'm so proud of you starting a new school all by yourself,' Mum says, coming over to kiss my forehead. Her hands are covered in breadcrumbs and she wipes them on her apron.

I wish she wasn't being so nice to me right now. I swallow and almost spill everything to her about the text message.

Almost.

Because every time I think about opening my mouth, I can't find the words. They get stuck in the back of my throat and then the longer I think about it, the harder it is to say them aloud.

'It's going to freeze tonight,' says Mum, who's

now back at the stove and hasn't noticed that anything is wrong. 'Better salt the planks and the deck.'

We all have jobs on the boat to make sure that everything gets done. One of mine is to make sure the deck is clear and not slippery.

I grab the salt bucket. As I step out on the deck my phone pings. I reach into my pocket and pull it out.

New Message

I open it.

Is that why your dad doesn't live with you? He couldn't face the stinky boat?

I drop the salt bucket and it topples over. I look around, my heart quickening, as if the person sending the messages could be nearby somewhere. The evening air is quiet and still. My stomach lurches and I feel sick. The words cut through me. I turn and run back inside, leaving the salt in a pile on the deck.

I throw myself down on my bed and take deep breaths, staring up at wooden slats on the ceiling.

How would anyone know about Dad?

I know I should tell Mum about this. What's stopping me?

She'll be so upset. She's fiercely protective of our boat life. I roll on to my side and imagine her storming up to school and making a big fuss.

That's the last thing I want. I need time to figure out who it is by myself.

But there's another thought that keeps creeping in, even though I'm trying to push it away.

What if Dad didn't want to live on a boat?
What if that's the reason he left?

Gwyon watched and listened and picked up things when she could, desperately trying to learn how to make the potion to save her brother. At night, she sneaked into the sorceress's study and read the potion lists and the spells. She stared into the glimmering glistening jars, some full of thick gloopy substances and some so thin you could almost see through them into other worlds. One sparkled as dark as a black hole.

Chapter Eight
Stars

'You're quiet again tonight, *mi amor*,' Mum says, checking on me later.

'I'm just tired,' I reply.

'Enjoying your new book?' asks Mum, nodding at my newest addition, lying next to me on my bed: *A Survival Guide to the Outdoors*. It was a present for my birthday. I already knew how to do all the knots in it. I wonder what Sophie or Aisha would think of the book and whether they'd find it weird. I bet neither of them know how to survive outdoors.

'Come and eat,' says Mum.

I nod and follow her out to the kitchen.

Enzo, Bryn and Aria are already sitting at the table with the safe in front of them.

'Still haven't figured it out?' I ask.

Bryn huffs loudly and folds his arms across his chest.

We try a different combination every night. Tonight, I try my birthday. The dial is still stiff to turn and the numbers click loudly as it spins. I pull on the door but it doesn't give. I shake my head.

'Maybe we can track down the original owner, or contact the manufacturer,' I say. 'Are there any markings on it?'

Bryn turns the safe upside down and shakes his head. 'Just these scratches.'

'I'll keep thinking,' I reply. 'We need to do some detective work.'

My mind turns back to the text message. I'm going to have to do some detective work on that too.

'Tonight is a meteor shower,' says Mum. 'Let's go up on the roof with some hot chocolate before bed and watch. We might see some shooting stars.'

So after dinner, we bring blankets and big cushions up to the roof and huddle up together, each of us clutching a mug of hot chocolate. Willow lies across all our feet. The sky glitters with stars. It's a half moon and there's hardly any light pollution. The boat shakes gently underneath us. Every now again a strong breeze bangs the boat against the towpath shoulder.

Bryn slides across the slippery roof, pirouetting in his socks.

'Don't knock over the hot chocolate,' says Mum.

'Can I have a marshmallow?' asks Aria.

'We don't have any marshmallows, *bebita*,' says Mum. She nods at the sky. 'Let's watch out for shooting stars.'

We clutch our warm mugs and crane our necks so that we can stare up at the sky. My neck aches but I keep staring, determined to see a shooting star. I know what I would wish for: to find out who the texter is.

'Those ones look like a marshmallow, all together,' says Aria.

Mum laughs. 'You've got marshmallows on the brain.'

'We can't go to bed until we've all seen a comet,' says Bryn, looking around at us sternly.

'That could be a while if you don't look up at the sky,' I reply.

'Do you think Dad's watching it too?' asks Aria.

'Maybe,' says Mum. 'He'll be back on Thursday. You can ring him and ask.'

'There's one!' says Enzo.

'Not fair!' says Bryn. 'I want to see one.'

'Look towards Orion,' says Mum. 'They're coming from over there.'

For a split second, so brief I might have imagined it, I see a glowing arc of bright light streak across the sky.

'There!' I shout.

'I saw it!' says Bryn.

'Me too!' says Enzo. His signs are lit up by the light of the moon.

'If I say I saw it does that mean we have to go to bed?' asks Aria.

Mum laughs and reaches over and ruffles her hair. 'Actually, Aria and Bryn,' she says, checking her watch, 'it's definitely your bedtime.'

'Cara always gets to stay up later than me,' says Aria, hands on hips.

'And Enzo gets to go to bed late too,' adds Bryn.

'That's because we're a whole lot older than you. I'm twice your age,' I say.

Aria pouts.

It's gone nine by the time Mum tucks them into bed and the stars have moved across the sky. Enzo takes my hand in his and squeezes it, the way we always say goodnight to each other, before following them inside. I decide to stay on the roof a bit longer by myself.

How do I find out who the number belongs to?

Lights in the windows of houses twinkle in the distance on the hill. I wonder what it would be like to live in a house. I've never really thought about it before. But right now it would make everything easier.

The mystery texter would have nothing to say to me.

Mum pokes her head out up on the roof. 'You OK up here?' she asks.

'Why do we have to live on a boat?' I ask quietly.

She climbs up and sits down cross-legged next to me. 'We don't *have* to. We choose to.'

'But why?' I ask.

'Being on a boat is special. We have the freedom to move if we want. Isn't that brilliant? And there's a beauty in hands-on living. And we get to be a part of this wonderful community.'

'Do you think we'll ever live in a house like everyone else?' I ask.

'Well we don't do something just because everyone else is doing it. Do you *want* to live in a house?'

'I'm fed up with having to explain to everyone . . .' I trail off, my words catching in the back of my throat.

'Did something happen at school?' asks Mum.

I shake my head.

'Are you worrying about anything?' Mum continues. 'Is it the work? Your new teachers?'

'It's not the work,' I reply.

We sit in silence for a while.

'It must be tough, not really knowing anyone there . . .' she tries again.

I nod my head.

'I promise you'll make new friends soon. I know it's hard and scary, but I also know that you are capable of handling it. You're strong.'

She's trying to make me feel better, but I feel like more and more of a failure. I'm not strong at all.

'Why don't you invite someone over next week?' she asks.

Mum doesn't understand.

I sigh. I'm tired of it all.

'When I'm out jogging and I feel like I can't run any more I tell myself, *Today I can do this, one step at a time. A camino largo, paso corto.* That might help you too. What do you think?' asks Mum, cocking her head to the side and staring at me. Her bushy hair falls from behind her ears.

'I just don't want to talk about it any more, OK?' I say.

She watches me sadly for a moment, then sighs. 'All right, *mi amor.* Good night.'

I nod, and she goes back inside.

Later, I huddle up in my bed, emotions still welling up inside me. It's cold tonight. The windows are already steamy and frosty. I pull my duvet tightly around me. When Mum comes to check on me, I close my eyes, pretending to be asleep.

I can feel her standing in the doorway for a few minutes and then she's gone, and I open my eyes again, staring into the darkness.

I realise there's a tiny bit of me that blames her for all of this. She's the reason we live on a boat. And if Dad left because he didn't want to live on a boat then that's her fault too.

I toss and turn in the little bed and, for the first time ever, my bedroom nook feels too small and cramped, as if it's closing in on me.

December 16th - Present Day

That night, my worst nightmare came true. Something happened that everyone who's ever lived on a boat dreads. We had prepared for it with safety checks, alarms and drills. But even though we did everything we were supposed to, we couldn't stop it.

People would come and visit the sorceress from far and wide to get potions for growing crops, fixing sore teeth and healing ailments. Each time the sorceress mixed a potion, Gwyon watched her, trying to gather what information she could, because she only had a year to save her brother and the weeks were going by.

Chapter Nine
Plank

I wake with a jolt. The fire alarm is blaring. And I can smell smoke. Willow barks, quick and urgent.

'Mum!' I shout.

She appears in the doorway, pulling on her shoes. 'It's a fire, Cara!' she calls. 'I've got Enzo, you get the twins.'

We've practised what to do in case of a fire over and over again, but now that it's not a drill my feet are frozen to the spot.

The feeling only lasts a split second.

I hurry into the twins' room. Aria's already helping Bryn down from his bunkbed. She coughs from the smoke.

'There's really a fire this time, isn't there?' shouts Bryn.

I nod and say, 'Hold my hand.'

All the while the alarm booms around us. I can see where the smoke is coming from now – it's the living room.

'Hurry,' says Mum, her voice tense. She is guiding Enzo. Aria runs up and clasps her hand.

Mum leads us towards the nearest exit at the front of the boat and then out to the deck. Outside it's pitch black except for the light streaming from the boat windows.

'Wait!' Bryn cries. His hand slips out of mine before I can grab tighter. 'I want to get the safe!'

He dashes back inside. Mum is ahead, guiding Aria and Enzo. She hasn't seen.

'Stop! Where are you going?' I yell. Bryn doesn't stop and I pelt after him down the steps.

Inside, all the lights are on and smoke has filled the sitting room. Flames curl up out of the flue pipe and reach for the wooden panels on the ceiling. There must be a hole in the pipe that's allowed the fire from the wood-burner to break out and spread. I know what could happen if the flames reach the back of the boat and the engine. The whole boat could explode.

There are noises all around. The sizzling of the flames on the wood. The relentless alarm. Mum shouting.

I can't think clearly. This happens sometimes. It's as if all the thoughts have been squashed inside my head, completely filling the space and my brain freezes while it sorts them all out. And until it does that, it lets me think about nice things like jellyfish floating in the sea or peanut butter being spread on bread.

We have to put the fire out or the whole boat could burn down.

'Cara!' shouts Mum, appearing at the top of the stairs. It jolts me and my thoughts catch up with the adrenaline rushing round my body. I see Bryn ahead of me and spot the safe lying on the sofa, close to the fire.

'You have to get out!' I yell at him. 'Forget about the safe.'

He hesitates, then turns and runs towards me, leaving the safe behind. I grab his arm and drag him up the stairs.

On the deck of the boat the cold fresh air hits me and I gulp it down. We shimmy along the outside of the boat, on the gunwales to the back where the plank is. Aria, Enzo and Willow are watching anxiously from the towpath.

'Careful on the plank,' says Enzo. He kneels and grasps the wood, making sure it doesn't wobble as Bryn steps on it. He shuffles along it, jumping on to the land when he's close enough. I spot the layer of frost covering the wooden plank and grip it with trembling fingers at this side.

I step on to the plank next and my foot immediately slides down it. I didn't expect it to be so slippery and I teeter for a moment before regaining by balance.

Lights are on in our closest neighbours, Jenny and Raj's, boat and they race towards us, shouting and carrying torches.

Frosty grass crunches under my feet as I leap from the end of the plank to the ground. My body shakes. Beads of ice glitter on the path.

Thick smoke billows from the chimney on the boat and sparks fly up into the sky.

'Everyone OK?' asks Raj, reaching us.

'The fire engines are on the way,' says Jenny, out of breath from rushing.

In the distance, I hear the sirens.

Mum's standing on the deck, staring back at the fire, her expression pained and worried.

'Do you need help?' Raj asks Mum.

'I want to put out the fire,' she shouts.

'Wait for the fire engines!' shouts Raj. 'Get on the bank.'

Mum nods. 'You're right.'

I pull Enzo, Bryn and Aria close. Aria squeezes my hand.

'You look freezing,' says Jenny. 'Let me get you some blankets.' And she darts off back to her boat.

In the distance, the sky is lit up by blue flashing lights. 'I'll go and meet the firefighters,' says Raj, urgently. 'I told them they'd have to park and walk.'

'Be quick,' says Mum.

He runs down the towpath.

Mum steps on the plank.

And then everything happens so quickly.

Mum walks down the plank, just like she does every day, but as she reaches the end, she slips and loses her balance.

I can't get my own body to move fast enough, to catch her and hold her before she falls. As she drops, she hits her head against the edge of the canal.

And then, with a splash that sends cold water spraying against my ankles, she is gone.

One day, a traveller from the north visited and bought a potion for earache. As the sorceress mixed his remedy, he told her about a legendary potion from his home. It was known as the most powerful elixir ever created, a single drop of which could make a person the strongest, wisest and mightiest in all the land. The sorceress's eyes grew wide with hunger.

Chapter Ten
Unknown

I'm frozen to the spot, but Willow jumps straight into the water after her.

'Mum!' cries Aria. Her cry sparks me into action. I dash to the edge and slide into the canal. I gasp as icy water touches my skin, drenching my clothes and making them heavy. I can touch the bottom with my feet until I step forwards and the ground disappears and I'm treading water. It's too dark and murky to see through. Dark shadows swarm around me.

Willow emerges, pushing Mum above the surface with her nose and doggie-paddling towards me.

I grab Mum and rest her head on my chest, hauling her to the edge by swimming with one arm. Willow swims beside me.

'Good girl, Willow,' I gasp. 'Good girl.'

Enzo, Aria and Bryn crouch at the water's edge.

'Help me lift her out!' I say, as I reach the side and am able to stand again. I try to keep my voice as calm as I can.

Enzo's face is pale. He bends, slides his hands under Mum's arms and pulls her on to the shore.

I climb out behind Mum, dripping water everywhere. She is sprawled on the path, her eyes closed and face pale.

I kneel in front of her. I put my ear over her

mouth and listen and feel for the movement of air. 'She's breathing.'

I let out a sob of relief.

'Which side is the recovery position?' I ask.

I can't remember.

Enzo's already turning Mum on to her left side for the recovery position, with her right knee bent. Willow helps him, nudging Mum with her snout.

'What happened?' Jenny rushes towards us, carrying blankets. She drops them and kneels by Mum.

'She slipped,' I say, my voice a trembling wave.

Jenny's immediately on the phone to the paramedics.

'She's going to be fine, isn't she?' asks Bryn.

'Of course,' says Jenny, one hand on Mum's wrist, checking her pulse. 'She's going to be just fine.'

Enzo gently strokes Mum's hair. An owl hoots overhead.

I squeeze Aria and Bryn's hands tightly in my own.

'Don't let go,' whispers Aria. Her face is streaked with tears.

'I won't,' I say, my voice cracking. 'I'm not going anywhere. We're all going to stay together.'

The next hour passes in a blur. Within minutes the towpath is full of firefighters. They carry huge fire extinguishers and douse the flames until the fire is out. A crowd of other boaters, woken up by the sirens and commotion, gathers to see if they can help.

The paramedics and police arrive next. They shine torches and drape metallic blankets on us. The paramedics ask us questions:

'What's your name, love?'

'Are you hurt?'

'Did your mother bang her head?'

Mum is taken away on a stretcher and we follow, Willow padding alongside us.

'I'll go with your mum in this ambulance,' says Jenny, kindly. 'Raj will go with you in the other one.'

The doors close behind Mum and the ambulance speeds off, siren blaring.

We pile in the next ambulance and sit in a line, shivering and shaking from the cold and the shock of it all. My clothes are still drenched and a paramedic covers me in a thick, warm blanket.

Willow jumps straight into the back of the ambulance with us. I see one of the paramedics hesitate.

'She's a service dog,' I say, pointing at Enzo's hearing aids. 'She has to come.'

The paramedic nods and closes the doors. Her dark hair is pulled back into a bun and she has a thick coat on over her dark-green uniform.

'I've never been in an ambulance before,' says Bryn.

The paramedic smiles at him. 'This is the first time we've ever had four kids and a dog in here all at once.'

'Mum always says we should stick together,' says Aria proudly.

The paramedic laughs. 'Your mother sounds very wise.'

Aria rests her head against Bryn's and we sit in silence for the rest of the ride, squeezing each other's hands. The ambulance ride seems endless.

Please, I think. *Please let Mum be OK.*

After meeting the traveller, the sorceress stopped assisting the people who came to her for help. She became obsessed with developing the potion that would make her the strongest, the wisest and the most powerful in all the land. In trying to discover the recipe, the sorceress made Gwyon work even harder than before, stirring and shaking new concoctions, day and night.

Chapter Eleven
Peril

At the hospital, the paramedics lead us inside. Everything is bright and sterile, and the entrance is filled with the scent of hand sanitiser. Willow jumps out and follows us in, wagging her tail.

A nurse takes over from the paramedics and, after talking to Raj, shows us to a room. I leave a trail of drips behind me. I squirm. My clothes are damp and uncomfortable.

'You wait here,' says one of the nurses. 'I'll get you some warm clothes and a hot drink.'

'I just want to find out how Mum is,' I say.

'I know, pet,' he says. 'Someone will be in to speak to you soon.'

'I'm sure it won't be long,' says Raj, trying to comfort us. 'Let's take a seat for now.'

My arms and knee are grazed and bleeding. I must have knelt on some glass or something sharp. I didn't feel it at the time but now it throbs. The nurse puts disinfectant on my cuts and they sting but I know it's important they're cleaned; the canal is full of all sorts of bacteria.

They give us all clean pyjamas to wear and I'm thankful to be out of my wet clothes.

'When can we see Mum?' asks Aria.

'Yeah! Where is she?' asks Bryn.

The nurse pulls out a chair and sits down in front of us. He leans forward, hands clasped together. 'Your mum is in intensive care,' he says.

Enzo looks at me, eyes filled with worry.

'She is stable,' the nurse goes on. 'The doctors have put her into a deep sleep to prevent any swelling in her brain. But we'll wake her up soon. And for now, she's sleeping soundly.'

The nurse turns to me. 'Do you have any other family we can contact? Your mum's parents?'

'No,' I shake my head. Grandma died a few years ago.

'But my dad lives in Wales. You can call him. I know his number.'

I've known his mobile number off by heart since I was seven.

After a little while the nurse returns. 'There's no answer. We'll keep trying.'

'Please can we see Mum?' I ask. 'Please.'

The nurse nods. 'Of course. I'm afraid you'll have to take it in turns to wait here with your dog. She's not allowed in intensive care.' He notices the dismayed look on our faces and adds, 'Maybe the dog could wait outside the hospital for a little while and that way you could all go in together. I can get her a water bowl?'

'I'll wait with Willow,' says Raj. 'And look, here's Jenny now.'

Jenny hugs each of us before we follow the nurse to see Mum. Willow whines as we leave.

Mum's in a room by herself. I gasp when I see her.

There are wires all over her chest. Beeps sound from the machines monitoring her.

'Mum,' says Aria. 'It's me.'

Mum, still and sleeping, doesn't respond.

'Why won't she wake up?' Aria asks, tears brimming in her eyes.

'She will,' the nurse replies. 'But now she needs to rest.'

'Can I hold her hand?' asks Bryn.

'Of course,' replies the nurse.

I want to rest my head on her shoulder but I'm scared to in case I hurt her. I rest my hand on top of Aria's instead.

We stay this way for what feels like hours, silent and listening to the beeps and sound of breathing. None of us knowing what to say. Every time I blink, I picture the icy plank, slippery, glistening in the light of the flames.

Gwyon asked time and time again if she could
learn how to make the potion that could heal
her brother. She knew that the months were
ticking by and soon it would be too late.

But the answer was always the same.

'Be patient,' the sorceress would say,
'I will teach you soon enough.'

Chapter Twelve
Patient

We fall asleep curled up in chairs and the space around Mum on the bed and don't wake up until a nurse, different from the one last night, walks into the room. The smell of toast and coffee follows her in.

'There's breakfast in the family room.' She gives us a warm smile. 'Go on, have something hot while it's there. There won't be an update for another hour or so.'

I wipe my eyes and glance at Mum. She looks exactly the same as she did last night, as if frozen in time.

At least she's no worse.

'Let's go and see what's there,' I say to the others, knowing that it's what Mum would want us to do. 'Just for a few minutes.'

Jenny is snoring on a chair outside with Willow by her feet. I shake her arm.

Willow jumps up and slobbers Enzo's face in kisses, tail racing back and forth.

'You're awake!' Jenny says, smiling at us. 'Raj had to go and check on the boats before work but I'm not going anywhere, OK? Have you eaten anything?'

'The nurse said we should now,' I reply.

None of us manage to eat much but Enzo saves a sausage for Willow, wrapping it in a napkin.

'Let's take her outside for a bit,' I say when we've finished as much as we can, filling a cup of water for her.

Aria looks nervously back at Mum's room.

'Jenny can stay with Mum while we walk Willow, right?' I look to Jenny and she nods.

I try and remember the way out, directing us through the long passages with glistening floors to where we came in. Eventually I spot the big entrance doors.

We walk Willow on the grassy verges around the car park.

'Do you think Mum will be OK?' asks Enzo.

'Of course,' I reply. 'They're taking great care of her.'

He nods but doesn't look reassured.

I know in my bones that she'll be back to her usual self in no time.

She has to be.

Willow lies down and stretches in the sun.

'I think she'd like to stay outside for a bit,' I say. 'What do you think?'

The others nod.

We tie Willow up on the grass by a fence. She rests her chin on her paws. I crouch in front of her. Her ears prick up and she meets my eyes. 'You have to wait here but we'll be back soon, OK? We're going to check on Mum.' I stroke her head from her wet nose to between the ears.

'Don't worry,' I say to Enzo. 'She knows it's only for a little while.'

He throws his arms around her before we leave.

Willow whimpers as we turn away and I hurry Enzo along, not wanting him to see her in distress.

I look back before we reach the entrance and she's laid back down.

It's just for a little while longer.

Dad will be here soon.

Enzo lets his hair fall in front of his face as we march back along the corridors.

Back in Mum's room, Jenny says that they've had an update from the police about *Newt*. 'She needs to be treated for smoke and some interior damage but structurally she's safe. Isn't that great? Some good news.' She smiles at us.

I try and smile back. I'm glad *Newt* will be OK but all I can think about is Mum.

Aria asks a nurse, 'Can she wake up yet?'

'It will be a few days at least,' says the nurse. 'But don't you worry, she's doing really well.'

I know her words are supposed to comfort us but they don't.

'Can I have a word, Cara?' asks a nurse, holding the door open for me.

I leave the others by Mum's bed and step outside.

'We haven't been able to get hold of your dad with the mobile phone number you gave us. Is there any other way we can get in contact with him?'

'That's his only number,' I say. 'His cabin doesn't have a phone.' Then I remember what he said the last time I spoke to him and my heart sinks. 'I think he's on a research trip near Snowdonia.'

She clicks her tongue. 'When will he be back?'

I try and remember how many days have passed since we spoke to him and when he said he was going to be back.

Thursday. And today is only Tuesday.

'He should be back by now,' I say, because I don't want them to give up calling him.

In the late afternoon, the nurse returns with another lady, who's clutching a clipboard and a plant pot with green stems sticking out from it. She's smiling at us.

'I brought your mum these,' she says, nodding towards the plant. 'They're crocuses.'

'Thanks,' I say. 'They're actually Mum's favourite.'

'My name's Bethan,' she says, placing the flowers down. 'I'm going to be your social worker.'

We glance at each with furrowed brows and worried expressions.

Why do we need a social worker?

'The thing is,' explains the nurse, 'I'm sure we'll track down your dad very soon. But in the meantime, you all need somewhere to stay.'

I blink, taking in what this means.

I don't want to stay with someone we don't know.

We all shake our heads at once.

'We're not leaving Mum,' I say.

'We can stay here. We don't take up much space,' adds Aria, opening her arms wide. 'I'm only this big, and look, I can fit on this chair here,' she finishes, gesturing.

'You won't even know we're here,' concludes Bryn.

'Even if you were all only this big,' says the nurse, putting her fingers one inch apart, 'then you'd still need to go home to rest. We'll take good care of your mum, don't worry.'

'We've found you a great foster carer,' says Bethan.

The words send a chill down my spine.

'We don't want to stay with a foster carer,' I say.

She sees my panic-stricken face. 'It's only temporary. Just until we can get hold of your dad.'

'Can't we stay with Jenny?' I ask, reaching for her hand.

'We're trying to make that happen,' says Jenny. 'But it could take a few days. They have to do an assessment of us and the boat before you can stay there. Besides, I'm sure we'll have contacted your dad in no time.'

'Can you try Dad again now,' I say. 'Please. Please try him again.'

It feels like the only thing I can get them to do.

I grip the twins' hands and as she goes to the phone I whisper under my breath.

Dad. Wherever you are. Please pick up.

But when she comes back in with a sympathetic smile and a shake of her head, I know he didn't answer.

And I don't know what else to do.

'Are we still going to be able to see Mum?' I ask.

'Of course,' replies Bethan. 'Every day.'

I wrap the twins in my arms at my sides and Aria rests her head against my shoulder.

'This isn't fair,' says Enzo, signing angrily.

'I know,' I say.

I don't know what else to say.

What would Mum do?

I try and hug him but he pulls away, stiff and upset.

Jenny says goodbye, squeezing us tight, and then we're being steered down the long corridors by the social worker.

Everything feels wrong.

'I've found you a lovely house for a few days,' says Bethan.

'A few days?' says Aria. 'Dad will be here tonight. Just you wait and see.'

'I've parked over there,' Bethan says, pointing to the left of the car park.

Enzo tugs at my sleeve.

Where's Willow?

The grassy verge we left her on is empty.

She's gone.

After six months, Gwyon confronted the sorceress.
'I've been working for you for longer than we agreed.
I have watched the pot and chopped and cooked and
cleaned for you. And you still haven't taught me the
potion. You broke your word and now I'm leaving.'

Chapter Thirteen
Willow

I whip my head around, my eyes flicking over cars, ambulances and people waiting at the bus stop. There are no dogs anywhere.

'Willow!' calls Aria.

'Where is she?' I ask.

'Who's Willow?' asks Bethan.

'Our dog. We left her here.'

'Did someone steal her?' asks Aria, her voice cracking.

Bryn drapes his arm around her shoulder, comforting her, his bottom lip trembling too.

I study the verge as if that will give a clue but there is just a lone crisp packet.

Enzo claps; Willow's been trained to respond. He waits a second then darts off, into the car park ahead of us, disappearing among the parked cars.

'Wait!' shouts Bethan. 'Don't run off. Come back.'

Swiftly, she ushers the rest of us back inside through the revolving doors. 'Wait here,' she says sternly. 'I'm going to find your brother.'

I turn and run to the reception desk. 'Has anyone seen a huge dog?'

'Pam, didn't you say something a big dog earlier?' a man calls to the back.

A friendly woman comes to the desk. 'Yes, I was worried about it. Big dog outside by itself like that for hours. I thought it might have been abandoned.'

'But we'd never abandon Willow,' says Aria, wiping her nose on her sleeve.

'What did you do?' I ask, despairingly. 'Where did she go?'

'Well, I called the council. They took her to the pound, dear.'

My insides plummet.

We rescued Willow from a shelter. We were supposed to get a service dog assigned to us for Enzo but we often volunteered as dog walkers at the shelter and that's where we found Willow as a puppy. She had a huge head, giant paws and wiry grey hair. Mum sent her for intensive special training and then Enzo worked extra hard to train her himself so that we could keep her. Mum was worried about her getting enough exercise but we got her to run alongside our bikes, up and down the towpath.

I remember how scared she looked in the cage at the shelter when we first met her and picture her back there.

'Sorry, my dears. She was your dog, was she?'

We all nod.

'Well, this is the number.' She hands a piece of paper to me.

Bethan returns with Enzo, who is hanging his head. I tell them what's happened.

'We'll ask Mrs Hobson – that's who is fostering you – if she can call when we get to her house,' Bethan says.

Aria taps my arm. 'If they've taken her back to the shelter then she'll think that we've abandoned her.'

'I know. We'll get her back soon.'

And I have no other choice but to go with this social worker for now. Things just keep getting worse. I've never felt so powerless. I feel like I'm letting everyone down. But I don't know what else to do.

The sun is low in the sky and it's already getting dark by the time we pull into a driveway half an hour later. I recognise the house in front of us. I always wonder about it when I cycle past. It stands by itself; a large cottage with a thatched roof and several chimneys. Ivy covers one half of the front and a rose arch leads up to the front door. Everything is pruned and weeded and too perfect. I've always wanted to know who lives here.

Inside is a big hallway. A tall lady walks towards us.

'Welcome,' she says, although she doesn't smile. 'I'm Mrs Hobson. You poor children have been through so much.'

We don't say anything and there's an awkward silence until Bethan speaks up.

'Well, I'll leave you to get settled in. I spoke to the fire department and they said that most of your belongings suffered smoke damage and will need to be washed or cleaned so I picked up some new clothes for you to wear. Your phone is in there too.' She looks at Mrs Hobson.

I take the bag of clothes. 'Thanks.'

'Which one's Enzo?' Mrs Hobson asks us.

Enzo waves in response.

'Let me know if there's anything you need,' she says, bending down in front of him and speaking terribly slowly and loudly, carefully pronouncing each word, the way people do sometimes when they find out he's hard of hearing.

We smirk and exchange glances, rolling our eyes.

'Can we check on Willow and get her back now, please?' I ask softly. 'She is Enzo's service dog,' I add, trying to get them to understand the sense of urgency.

'Of course,' says Bethan. She turns to Mrs Hobson. 'Their dog was taken to the shelter. Would you mind ringing and checking on her?'

'I'll ring them now,' says Mrs Hobson, taking the piece of paper with the number on it from me.

'Thank you,' I say with relief, tired of fighting to keep us all together.

Bethan gives us each a hug.

'Here's my number,' she says, handing me her card. 'I'll check on you soon.' She leaves, shutting the door behind her.

Meanwhile, Mrs Hobson goes into the next room to make the call. I try and stand close to the door, so that I can listen to the conversation, but I can only hear her distorted voice.

After a few minutes, Mrs Hobson returns. 'Willow's fine. I've explained the situation. They're looking after her at the shelter and are going to keep her there until you can all go home.'

'But we need to get her back,' I say, confused.

She gives a tight smile. 'My son is allergic to dogs. I couldn't possibly allow a pet in the house.'

'She's more than a pet,' I say. 'She's a service dog and we need her.' I stumble over my words, unable to believe that Mrs Hobson is stopping us from seeing Willow.

Mrs Hobson shakes her head. 'Out of the question, I'm afraid,' she says, as though that is that. 'Let me show you to your room.'

We stand there, silently taking everything in.

'We'll figure something out.' I sign secretly to Enzo, Bryn and Aria. 'We'll get her back somehow.'

Enzo looks empty without Willow by his side, as if a part of him is missing. I picture her padding across the floor and resting her giant head on his legs, and know that it would instantly comfort him and the rest of us. Without Mum here, we all need Willow more than ever.

We follow Mrs Hobson through the house. It is cold, big and damp. We walk on flagstone floors under old wooden beams with spiders' webs clinging to the corners. Knitted blankets hang over the back of the chairs.

'We only heat a few rooms at this time of year. These other doors stay shut,' says Mrs Hobson, showing us round the house. 'This is my son's room. He's at football but he'll be back later. This is where you'll be sleeping.'

Mrs Hobson opens two doors next to each other with identical twin beds in each room. Long curtains drape over the breezy windows. The same faded wallpaper covers every wall.

'Enzo and Bryn can stay in here and Cara and Aria can sleep in this one.' She gestures that I'll be in the room on the right. 'And don't worry if you hear some noise early in the morning; Mr Hobson has to leave for work at five tomorrow.'

We all file back into the kitchen. I glance at the clock. It's already four thirty in the afternoon. It feels as if no time has passed since last night when we were sitting on the roof of the boat, but at the same time it feels as if it's been an eternity.

'You must be famished,' Mrs Hobson says. A microwave pings, 'The lasagne is ready.'

She lifts it out of the microwave and places it in front of us along with some salad.

'Anyone hungry?' I ask.

Everyone gazes up at me with tired eyes and shakes their heads.

'You must eat,' says Mrs Hobson, doling out steaming portions.

We all sit and push the food around our plates. I wish I could ring Dad myself and get us all out of here. I search the bag Bethan gave me for my mobile. My fingers close around its cold shape and I lift it out. The phone got soaked when I jumped into the canal and was completely dead. A nurse at the hospital took it apart and dried off all the pieces. I wonder if it still works.

'Do you have a charger, please?' I ask Mrs Hobson.

She squints at it. 'I think you have the same brand as my son. Let me see.' She returns with one and hands it to me.

Aria's head falls to the side as she drifts off to sleep, dropping on to Bryn's shoulder. As soon as one of them falls asleep, it's contagious to the other. Bryn's eyes begin to droop too.

'I know it's early but I think it's bedtime,' says Mrs Hobson. 'You've must not have slept much during the past day.'

I plug my phone in, hoping that it will turn on after I charge it.

I help the other kids get undressed and into bed, then brush my teeth and lie down myself. But I can't sleep. Instead, I toss and turn, thinking about Mum and Willow. Mrs Hobson has promised to wake me if there's any news. Every time I close my eyes, images of the plank flash into my head; the smooth wood covered in glistening frost.

It's freezing in our bedroom, even with a duvet, and I wrap myself up in it.

After a while I hear the rustle of Aria moving in bed and then the tip-tap of her footsteps on the floorboards.

'Can I sleep with you?' she asks.

'Of course,' I say.

She climbs up and rests her head on the pillow next to me. Her steady rhythmic breathing calms my racing heart.

The sorceress didn't want Gwyon to leave. She needed
Gwyon's help to make the new, powerful potion.
The sorceress had discovered that Gwyon was skilled
at finding the ingredients she needed in the forest.

'Wait,' the sorceress said. 'If you help me
with this last potion then I promise you I
shall tell you how to save your brother.'

Gwyon agreed to stay. She had to try one last time.

Chapter Fourteen

Stuck

We're woken up by a knocking on our door at six am.

'Time to wake up!' calls Mrs Hobson. 'Get dressed – there's breakfast on the table.'

As Aria slowly wakes up, I try my phone. The screen flashes on.

'Yes,' I say. I immediately press Dad's contact. It goes straight to his voicemail.

I leave a message explaining what has happened, then send him a text.

Urgent. Ring me as soon as you get this.

Aria and I pull on our new clothes. Mine feel scratchy and uncomfortable.

'I don't want to go down there,' says Aria.

I hold out my hand. 'I'll be with you. And Bryn and Enzo will be there.'

She nods and takes my fingers. 'OK.'

I stop when we reach the bottom of the stairs.

Standing in the hallway is Keaton from school, the boy who sniggered during my English presentation. He's wearing a hoody with the hood up, gelled but messy dark hair poking out. I groan softly. The last thing I need is people at school finding out about this. In all the worry about Mum I hadn't even thought about school and the text messages but suddenly everything comes flooding back.

'What are you doing here?' I ask, glaring at him frostily.

What if it was him that sent the text messages?

'What do you mean?' he asks. 'I live here.'

Out of all the houses, it had to be his.

The son with allergies. So he's the reason Willow's not with us too. A ball of anger gathers in my chest.

'I'm sorry about your mum,' he says awkwardly, after a moment's silence. 'I'm sure she'll get better soon.' He turns to Aria. 'I'm Keaton.'

'Breakfast!' calls Mrs Hobson.

'We'd better go,' says Keaton, glancing at his mobile. 'Don't want to be late for school.'

'You go on ahead, I'll just be a second,' I say. I have a sudden idea. I don't think Keaton is the one sending me nasty texts — he's never paid me that much attention — but now would be the perfect time to make sure. I take out my mobile and dial the number of the texter. If it's Keaton, his phone will ring. I watch him through the crack in the kitchen door while I listen to the ring tone. He doesn't check his phone.

Maybe it's not him.

'What are you doing?' asks Aria, turning back and tugging on my sleeve.

'Just trying Dad again,' I say. 'Come on, let's go.'

Enzo and Bryn are already sitting at the kitchen table next to Keaton. Mrs Hobson moves between the fridge and the stove.

Behind them, on the wall, is a giant whiteboard and on it in neat handwriting is a schedule.

4pm. Homework.

5.30pm. Dinner and dishes.

6.30pm. Bath.

8.00pm. Bed time.

9.00pm. Lights out.

I catch myself pulling a face as I read it and try to soften my expression before Mrs Hobson notices.

Enzo jiggles his left knee up and down, fidgeting. I can tell he's worried about Willow. He hasn't spent a day apart from her since we rescued her.

'No elbows on the table,' says Mrs Hobson as she serves us bowls of porridge.

We all lift our arms from the table.

I take a spoonful of porridge and gag. It's salty. I've never had salty porridge before and I don't like it.

Aria takes a bite too and screws her face up in disgust.

'Do you have any honey?' I ask.

'Or raisins?' asks Bryn. 'I love raisins.'

'I don't have either right now,' Mrs Hobson replies.

To my surprise, Keaton's wolfing his down.

Mrs Hobson passes us plates with white gloop on them.

'What's this?' asks Bryn.

'It's scrambled eggs,' replies Mrs Hobson.

'But eggs are yellow,' says Aria.

'Oh, Keaton can't eat egg yolks,' says Mrs Hobson.

I'm about to say, 'Even if they're on somebody else's plate?' but I stop myself. Mrs Hobson is my direct line of communication to Mum and Willow. So instead I say, 'Everything looks delicious. Thank you.'

'You're most welcome,' she replies.

But still none of us touch the food.

Aria looks at me and whispers, 'I bet he's not even allergic to dogs.'

'This is all we're having for breakfast,' says Mrs Hobson, looking pointedly at our still-full plates and bowls. 'So I suggest you eat it. For those of you not going to school today, lunch will be at served promptly at 12pm.'

'I don't want to go to school today,' says Bryn. 'I just want to see Mum.'

'We all do,' I say.

'All right. We'll go after I've dropped Keaton off at school,' replies Mrs Hobson.

This cheers Aria and Bryn up.

I watch Keaton happily wolfing down his eggs. 'You don't actually think this tastes good, do you?' I whisper.

'You get used to it,' he replies.

'Do you get lonely in this big house without brothers and sisters?' Aria asks Keaton, shivering and wrapping her arms around her. I hush her.

'Have you ever been on a boat?' asks Bryn.

'Do you wish you lived on one?' asks Aria.

I rub my hand over my eyes, imagining Keaton laughing about this with his friends later at school.

'Oh goodness,' says Mrs Hobson. 'That's a lot of questions.'

'Mum says that we should never be afraid to ask questions,' says Aria. 'We ask her loads.'

'Is that right?' says Mrs Hobson. 'And I suppose your mother knows all the answers too?'

The twins laugh.

'As if,' says Aria.

'If Mum doesn't know the answer, she says we should write the question down and put it in a box. Then we can figure it out together,' explains Bryn.

'Usually we go to the library,' adds Aria. 'You can always find an answer there.'

I glance at Enzo. He hasn't even tasted the porridge; he's just sitting there, leaning his head in his hand, staring at the table.

I reach across and squeeze his hand.

'We'll get Willow back somehow,' I say. 'I promise.'

After breakfast, Mrs Hobson drops Keaton off at school before taking us to the hospital to see Mum.

'We still haven't been able to get hold of your dad,' says a nurse at the front desk of the intensive care unit. 'I'm sorry. We'll keep trying.'

I swallow and nod.

'Let's go and see Mum,' I say.

We spend the day with her, holding her hand and telling her all about Mrs Hobson's house while she sleeps. The doctor arrives in the afternoon to update us. 'There's been no change but she's stable, which is good news.'

When Mrs Hobson arrives to take us back to the house that afternoon, we still haven't been able to contact Dad.

'I don't want to go,' says Aria, scowling and crossing her arms.

'Especially not without Willow,' says Enzo.

'I know,' I reply. 'But we have to go with her for now.'

Outside, as we're walking across the car park, a voice shouts, 'Hey!' I spin around and spot the reporter that interviewed us for the news the other day. 'You were part of the boat clean-up crew. Was it your boat that caught fire?'

I nod.

'I'm so sorry,' she replies. 'Can I ask you a few questions about it?'

'We're not really in the mood to be famous today,' says Aria.

'I can't identify any names but I'd be happy to be interviewed,' says Mrs Hobson, jumping in. 'I'm looking after them while their mum's in hospital.'

'That would be great,' says the reporter.

We stand in the background while Mrs Hobson explains about the fire, how we don't have anywhere else to go and how worried we are about our mum. With each word I can feel my heart sink lower. It's clear we're stuck with Mrs Hobson, and it's feeling harder and harder to see a way out.

December 16th – Present Day

It was in that moment that I realised we needed a plan, something to keep our hopes up and keep us together as a family. I didn't know what it was going to be but I knew I needed to come up with it quickly.

Through her experiments, the sorceress had learnt
that to make the most powerful potion in the land,
she had to use leaves from every type of tree, and
foliage from every plant in the forest. And so,
she sent Gwyon out to gather the ingredients.

Chapter Fifteen

Quest

That evening Enzo hardly touches his food. It's the leftover lasagne from last night, now soggy with grey pieces of pasta. I can feel the sadness in Enzo's drooped posture and vacant expression. Mr Hobson eats with us — he is a short, quiet man with dark hair.

There has to be something I can do.

'Can I go to the bathroom?' I ask Mrs Hobson.

She nods, sitting opposite me.

Outside, I stand in the hallway, trying to think. I look up and see the closed doors we're not allowed to go through. I open them. I don't really know what I'm searching for, but it feels powerful, like at least I'm doing something.

One of the doors leads down to a basement. I pull the switch on and follow the steps. It's mainly empty, just a big room that smells damp. Two kayaks lie in the corner. A thick layer of dust covers everything. Clearly no one has been down here in some time.

It's the perfect place to hide a big dog.

Back at the dinner table I catch Enzo's eye and sign at everyone. 'I have a plan. We're going to rescue Willow.'

Aria and Bryn beam.

I look up at Keaton and Mr and Mrs Hobson and grin. They have no idea what I just said.

Before bed, I gather everyone in my and Aria's room. 'The animal shelter is just round the corner. And if we can get Willow, we can hide her here.'

'We can't hide Willow here,' says Enzo. 'She's huge.'

'Aha,' I say, raising a finger and pretending to be a detective. 'You might think that, but this house is huge too. And guess what? I found a basement. We could keep her there. It will only be for another day or two anyway, right?'

Enzo's eyes light up. 'How do we get her back?' he signs excitedly. 'The shelter will want a grown-up to sign her out.'

'We break her out,' I say. 'Is everyone in?'

Enzo nods.

'Yes!' says Aria. 'I miss her so much.'

'Me too!' says Bryn, dancing on the spot.

'What will we feed her?' asks Enzo. 'And how will we walk her?'

I pause. 'We can sneak out and walk her at night. And I saw some chicken in the fridge — maybe we can feed her that.' I wish I could plan further ahead but we'll have to figure it out as we go. 'For now, let's just get her back here with us,' I say, trying to sound reassuring.

I'm done with waiting.

It's time to take control.

I lie in bed listening until I hear the creak of the house as Mr and Mrs Hobson go to bed. I wait a bit longer, then check my phone and see it's eleven o'clock. Everything's silent except for the wind blowing through the cracks under the window and an owl hooting outside.

I creep to the other bedrooms and wake everyone else.

'It's time,' I say. 'Let's go.'

Enzo rubs his eyes and nods. Bryn and Aria hold hands as they follow me through the dark hallways.

Earlier, when Mr and Mrs Hobson were watching television, I'd gathered two torches, some string to use as a lead for Willow, and a pair of scissors in case we need to cut a tag off Willow or something like that. I couldn't think of anything else we might need.

We stop in the hallway and slip on the coats hanging from the hooks, the ones the social worker gave us. I gently try the front door, turning the handle, but it's locked and I can't find a key.

'What now?' mouths Aria.

'Stay still,' I whisper, holding my finger to my lips. I look around, my gaze landing on the bay windows in the living room. The key to one of the windows is still in its lock. Relieved, I twist the key and push the window open. Cold air rushes in.

'How are we going to get back in?' asks Bryn.

'We'll leave the window open,' I reply. 'Just a crack so that we can pull it open again from the outside.'

'What if we get lost?' asks Aria.

'I know the way,' I say.

'It's going to be the great big dog break-out. I can't wait until we tell Mum,' says Bryn.

'Now, who wants to go first?' I ask.

'I'll go,' says Enzo. He pulls himself up and drops down on to the rose bed on the other side of the window. 'Ouch. Watch out. It's prickly.'

'I'll help you over,' I say to the twins. The windows are just high enough for them to need a hand climbing over.

I form a step with my fingers interlocked for them to use.

But then we hear a voice that makes us freeze.

'What are you doing?' asks Keaton. He flicks the light switch on. He's wearing tracksuit bottoms, a fleece and a hat.

'Shhh,' I say. 'Turn the light off.'

He stares at us. 'Are you running away? I wouldn't do that if I were you. Mum will *not* be happy.'

Enzo stands on the other side of the window.

'We're just going for a midnight stroll,' I say, trying to sound casual. 'It's a family tradition once a week. Really grounding. Don't you do that too?'

'You go for a family stroll looking like that?' he asks, nodding towards Bryn and Aria. I hadn't even noticed that they'd tied pairs of tights around their eyes and cut holes in them like bandits.

'Yes,' I say airily. 'You can dress however you want.'

There is a pause while he looks at us. 'What are you really doing?' he asks after a minute. 'Committing a crime? Going back to your boat? Trying to see your mum?'

'Wrong, wrong and wrong,' I say.

'Bet I'm not,' he says.

'Yeah you are, we're going to get our dog back, so there,' says Aria. Her hand immediately flies to her mouth, but it's too late.

Keaton gazes outside at the darkness. 'You're going to get your dog? Can I come with you?' he whispers. 'I never get to do stuff like this.'

'You won't tell your mum?' I ask, surprised.

He shakes his head. 'Definitely not.'

'Aren't you allergic to dogs?' asks Aria.

'That's what my mum says,' replies Keaton. 'But I honestly don't even remember the last time I was around one. So I don't know.'

Enzo signs at me through the window that he doesn't trust him.

'Me neither,' I sign back at him. 'But we don't really have a choice.'

'Then let's go already,' says Enzo. 'It's cold.'

I frown, thinking.

Keaton's acting like he wants to help, but I still don't want him tagging along. Then again, getting Willow out is my priority right now and he could be useful.

'OK,' I say to Keaton. 'You can come.'

Inside my head, I add, *you'd better be telling the truth about keeping your mouth shut.*

Gwyon reminded the sorceress that she'd promised to help her save her brother if Gwyon helped with this final potion. The sorceress agreed and told her three of the five ingredients needed to make the potion to heal her brother: a ballerina waxcap, a handful of feverfew flowers and six stinging nettle leaves. She promised that soon she would tell her the other two items.

Chapter Sixteen

Brave

Outside, we all make our way down the dark lane, which is lit up by only a few streetlights. Our shoes echo against the tarmac. We walk for a while in silence, until Bryn finally breaks it.

'Are you allergic to all animals?' he whispers to Keaton.

'I'd be so sad if that happened to me,' says Aria.

'I don't think so,' Keaton says, 'But I've never been around many animals. Mum says they carry germs.'

'What about cats?' asks Bryn.

'I've never got close to one,' replies Keaton.

'No way. What about a hamster?'

'Same,' says Keaton. 'Anyway, we've been walking for ages. I thought you said the shelter wasn't far.'

'I've only ever cycled it,' I reply. 'It seems a lot quicker on a bike.'

Leaves rustle and I wrap my coat around me. Headlights shine up the road as a car approaches. We jump behind a tree and stay still until it's passed.

I take hold of Aria and Bryn's hands to keep them from wandering too far off course. There are deep ditches on the sides of the roads, not to mention the river running below us.

Bryn yawns noisily. 'How much further?'

'We're close, I promise. Look, there's our school,' I say, directing the last bit at Keaton.

'Great,' says Keaton. 'As if I don't see enough of it in the day.'

I study him through the darkness, surprised that he doesn't seem to like school either. He has tons of friends.

'My feet are wet,' complains Aria.

'Almost there,' I say, feeling annoyed with everyone's grumbling. 'The shelter is behind the school. Come on.'

Flood lights shine on the shelter building. In front of it is a tall fence with a locked gate. I remember the layout from when we used to walk the dogs.

'They'll be keeping her in the back kennels because she's so big,' I say.

'What are you going to do with the dog after you've rescued her?' asks Keaton.

We all glance at each other.

'Bring her home,' I say.

'Not to *my* home though, right?' says Keaton.

'Just for a few days,' I reply.

'Oh no. That is definitely not happening. No way. My parents will have a fit.'

'Where did you think we were going to bring her?' I ask.

'I don't know. I thought you were going to set her free or something.'

From the other side of the fence, I hear a heart-breaking howl. Willow.

She knows we're here.

'No way,' I say, scrunching my face up in disapproval. 'She's part of the family. We'd do anything to get her back.'

Keaton nods in the direction of the fence. 'I can see that.'

I've been so distracted by Keaton's comments that I haven't noticed Enzo climbing up and scaling the fence. By the time I look up he's already at the top. Although he's not that tall, Enzo has broad shoulders and strong arms.

Enzo is an experienced climber. He goes to the climbing gym every other week to practise bouldering or belaying. But seeing him up there still sends my heart into my mouth.

'Be careful,' I say under my breath, although I know there's nothing I can do now.

Moments later, he lands with a thud on the other side.

Dogs bark.

Someone's going to hear soon.

I turn to Keaton. 'Wait here and stand guard with Aria and Bryn.'

He nods.

I slip my trainers off — they're too big to fit in the holes of the fence — and climb after Enzo. I'm not a good climber like him but I feel confident after watching him do it. The metal wire digs into the skin on my toes. I jump down, catch up with him and we tiptoe towards the kennels at the back. The barking crescendos in volume.

I pass one of the torches to Enzo and we each take an aisle of cages. After a few minutes of shining my torch in dog's faces, I spot Willow. She scratches against the door of the cage when she sees me. I unclip the lock by lifting the metal pin out and open it.

She immediately bounds straight into my arms, tail wagging at supersonic speed. When Enzo runs over to us, Willow practically knocks him over in her excitement to see him.

I want to bury my head in Willow's fur and let her warmth help me forget everything about the last few days, but I know we need to get out of here before someone comes to investigate all the barking, so I sign to Enzo that we need to go. Together we pass the other sorrowful eyes watching us, the poor dogs wondering why they aren't also being taken for a walk.

'I'm sorry,' I say to them. 'I'm sure someone will come for you soon.'

'How are we going to get her out?' asks Enzo.

I look around with my torch. There's a gate behind the buildings. 'Over there,' I say, and we hurry over. It's only closed by a bolt lock on the inside. The gate creaks as we push it open.

We pick up our speed and jog around the outside to the front, where the others are waiting.

'That,' says Keaton, backing away from Willow, 'is not a dog. It's practically a horse.'

'Not a horse. Maybe a Shetland pony,' says Aria.

'Let's get out of here,' I say.

Willow trots beside us, occasionally licking our hands. She's so happy to be back with us that she's staying right by our sides. I haven't even needed to make her a lead. I feel stronger having her here with us. If Mum can just get better then we can all go back to the way things were before.

I stop suddenly.

'Where are my shoes?' I ask, realising I left them by the gate. 'I'll have to go back for them.'

'Not now, look,' says Keaton. We watch as a car pulls into the shelter. 'We can come back for them tomorrow.'

We hurry up the road, away from the shelter as quickly as possible. Soon I have a stitch in my side and my feet hurt from the rough ground. The wind roars through the trees and it begins to drizzle. I wipe the rain off my face with my sleeve.

Finally, we make it back to the house.

I freeze.

There's a big van parked directly outside that

I'm sure wasn't there before.

I stick my arm out to halt the others. Movement catches my eye at the window of the house.

There's someone, dressed in all black, standing beside the window we left open.

Gwyon was used to gathering ingredients but the sorceress had never requested so many different things before. Gwyon didn't like taking so much from the forest but eventually she managed to find everything — except for one ingredient. The rarest plant that existed. The lungwort lichen.

Chapter Seventeen

Breakout

I usher everyone behind a parked car further down the street. We crouch low in the shadows, watching the house. Our breaths are short and sharp.

'I think someone's burgling your house,' I say.

I peek out from behind the car and watch the burglar peering in through the window.

Keaton stares at me helplessly. 'What do we do?'

'Do you have a phone? We need to call the police.'

'It's inside,' says Keaton.

'Mine too,' I say, annoyed with myself for not bringing it.

Sensing the fear racing through my bones, Willow crouches and growls.

'That van wasn't there when we left, was it?' says Bryn.

'It must be their getaway van,' says Keaton.

Enzo reaches into my coat pocket and pulls out the scissors. He bends down and creeps towards the van.

I cover my mouth with my hand, wanting to shout at him to come back but not wanting to alert the burglar to our existence.

I glance at the house and see the burglar inspecting the open window.

Enzo crouches by the front tyre. I can't see

what he's doing. There's a quiet hissing from the wheel and I realise he must be loosening the valve to let the air out. He does the same thing with the other three tyres and comes back.

'Where did you learn to do that?' I ask.

'I read about it. They'll be flat in an hour.'

'I've memorised the number plate,' whispers Bryn.

I raise an eyebrow at Bryn, impressed with his detective work. Then I risk a look at the house. The figure is pulling open the window now, and raising a leg up towards the ledge.

'He's going inside,' I whisper.

'I need to stop him,' says Keaton, standing. 'My mum and dad are in there!'

He steps out from behind the car.

'You can't go in there now,' I hiss at him. 'The burglar's right there! There might be someone else in the van. They'll see you.'

He ignores me and starts towards the house. Bryn runs after him, catching his sleeve, trying to stop him.

The figure at the window pauses. Keaton freezes, but it's too late.

The burglar must have sensed his movement because, halfway through the window, he stops and turns his head. Keaton and Bryn are clearly illuminated by a streetlight. A mask covers the burglar's face but I see his eyes glittering.

Suddenly, he jumps down from the ledge and charges at Keaton and Bryn. The wind roars and a green scarf billows out behind his bulky coat.

I dash towards them with Enzo, Aria and Willow close behind me.

Everything happens so quickly I hardly know what's going on.

The burglar grabs Bryn and lifts him into the air. Bryn's legs thrash back and forth.

'Help!' screams Bryn.

The burglar strides forward and opens the back of the van, sliding Bryn inside with a thump.

I run and leap in after him, trying to reach Bryn and pull him back out.

Behind me, the burglar grabs Aria by the arms and pushes her inside too.

She crashes into me, knocking me down.

'Get off her!' I punch and kick at the burglar.

He lets go and stands back before slamming the van doors. The lock clicks shut from the outside.

I rattle the handle.

It's locked.

'Let us out!' shouts Aria.

I yell and bang on the door, making as much noise as possible, willing someone to hear us.

Enzo and Keaton are outside. Enzo has Willow

with him. At least there's that.

'Are you hurt?' I ask them.

They shake their heads.

I realise the back of the van has a row of seats. The engine starts with a shudder and the van screeches away.

'Enzo let the air out of the tyres,' Bryn says miserably. 'Does that mean we'll crash?'

'I don't know,' I reply.

'Find a seatbelt,' I say to them both. We feel around the seats in a row and I fasten theirs and then mine.

There's a metal grate separating the back of the van from the driver. I can see the back of his head and his scarf.

'Let us out!' I shout towards him.

No answer.

'What do you want?' I try again. 'Where are you taking us?'

'Where is it?' he asks. His voice is syrupy but I can feel the anger seeping out from him.

'Where's what?' I shout. It's hard to hear him over the rumbling engine and windscreen wipers.

'The safe!' he shouts. 'I saw you on TV with it. I know you have it.'

'I don't know!' I shout, confused. I think back to the last time I saw the safe when Bryn went to grab it during the fire. There was smoke and the alarm and I know Bryn didn't take it. So much has happened since then that it hasn't even crossed my mind until now.

'Stop lying,' he yells, glancing back at us. 'I saw you with it. And now you're going to give it to me.'

That's when I realise we're flying down the road towards the canal.

He continues, his voice shrill and loud. 'I've searched that boat of yours as best I can and found nothing. I know you've got it on there somewhere.'

I glance at Bryn. The safe should still be on the boat.

'You're a meanie,' says Aria to the driver.

'What's in it?' I ask. 'Why do you want it so much?'

He says nothing.

'How do we know that he'll even let us go once he does have the safe?' whispers Aria.

Suddenly, the van shudders and veers to the side of the road. Sparks fly. The tyres have deflated – it must be the bare metal on the wheels hitting the tarmac. A screeching noise sounds as the burglar slams on the brakes.

We're thrown forward then back as the seatbelts catch us.

The van stops.

My heart races.

We're stuck in the back of a van with an angry burglar.

What do we do now?

The lungwort lichen's curly leaves grew on rotting wood. But not a tree in the forest had any. Every day Gwyon searched everywhere for it, and every day the sorceress grew angrier and angrier when she returned empty-handed.

Chapter Eighteen
Circumvent

'Everyone OK?' I whisper.

Shadows from the streetlights outside streak across their faces.

'I think so,' says Aria. Her voice shakes.

'Me too,' says Bryn.

The burglar opens the driver's door and stumbles out. He leaves his door open and goes to examine the front of the van. He shakes his head when he sees the flat tyres, muttering, 'Stupid bad luck. Every time.'

I undo my seatbelt and try the door handle, wondering whether we can make a run for it. It's locked. I shove at the metal grill between the front and back seats and it rattles but doesn't budge. The burglar pauses for a moment, before walking to the side of the van, out of sight.

'Don't worry,' I say, trying to hide the panic in my voice. 'Enzo will get help.'

'My arm hurts,' says Aria.

Her wrist is red where he grabbed her. I rub her skin gently.

Bryn whispers, 'Shouldn't Keaton have called the police by now? Where are the sirens?'

I crawl to the front of the van and stare at the driver's seat. The keys hang in the ignition. I try to stick my hand through the metal squares but only two fingers fit through.

I yelp. A pair of eyes are staring up at me from the driver's doorway. Then I realise it's Enzo.

His cheeks are flushed from running. He must have followed us here. We didn't get very far before the tyres blew. Willow is beside him.

'Grab the keys,' I say, pointing.

He reaches in for them and pulls them out of the ignition.

The van engine shuts off and the headlights dim.

'What's going on?' asks the burglar, striding back to the front of the van.

Enzo ducks out of sight.

'Undo your seatbelts,' I say urgently to the twins. 'We're getting out of here.'

The locks click. Enzo has done it.

I turn the handle and push the door open, hard.

The burglar is on the ground, wrestling Enzo, trying to prise the keys out of his hand. As I watch, Willow leaps on top of the burglar, grabs his coat in her mouth and pulls him off Enzo.

I turn and help Aria and Bryn out of the van.

'Run!' I shout.

Enzo darts into the hedgerow, diving through the bushes.

He helps us through after him.

The burglar throws Willow off, picks himself up and dashes after us. Willow turns and snarls at him, showing all her teeth, and he stops uncertainly, allowing us to scramble through the bushes, Willow hurrying after us.

Keaton is waiting the other side of the hedgerow, his expression worried. 'Come on,' he whispers. 'Hurry.'

We run into the darkness of the night.

It takes me a minute to get my bearings. Everything is bathed in silver whispers of light from the moon. In a split second I realise where we are. If we go through the field to our left, we'll pop out on the towpath, just a bit down from *Newt*.

'Follow me,' I hiss.

We run as fast as we can, wading through stinging nettles and leaping over cow pats and puddles of mud.

I can't hear anyone following us. I glance behind just to be sure. 'Where are the police?' I ask Keaton breathlessly. 'Where are your parents?'

'I didn't wake them,' he says. 'Enzo took off after you straight away and I followed without thinking.'

I don't have the breath to tell him what I think of that plan.

'I should have.' He shakes his head. 'I can't keep running much longer.'

'Let's just get to the boat!' I say, out of breath. 'It's too risky to go back to yours now. He'll catch us again.'

Aria takes his hand in hers and pulls him along.

We reach the end of the field and crawl through a bush on our hands and feet. I feel the prickly rash from the stinging nettles and the brambles. My heart races. The towpath is the other side of the bush. We're nearly there. Once we're on the boat we can start the engine and cruise away. He won't be able to catch us then.

As long as Newt's engine still works.

Willow bounds ahead, happy to be home. I spot *Newt* in the distance. As we get closer I see one of the windows has been smashed in.

I climb aboard and realise the whole boat has been turned upside down. Our furniture is everywhere. There is still a smell of smoke.

I step inside the cockpit, where the tiller is. It's enclosed by glass windows, our tiny little greenhouse. He's searched in here too but most of the plants are still upright.

Everyone follows me aboard and squeezes into the cockpit next to me. Picking up a succulent plant, I dig in the soil for the spare key. I find it. I wish and hope that the engine hasn't been damaged by the fire in any way. 'Here we go,' I say twisting the key in the ignition. The engine chugs loudly, then settles down to its usual rhythmic sound.

'Yes!' says Bryn. 'Go, *Newt*.'

I sigh with relief. Now we have a chance to escape.

After weeks of searching, Gwyon finally found the bright-green lichen, growing around the base of an oak tree, like a frilly skirt.

She bent down and picked just one leaf.

Chapter Nineteen
Escape

'I'm going to pull the mooring pins up!' I shout. I leave the boat in neutral and grab the hammer we use to prise the pins out of the ground. I leap on to the bank and yank them from the soil.

I don't bother to untie the rope from the mooring pins, just chuck them on board. They hit the deck with a clatter.

Leaning against the side is the wooden plank. The one Mum slipped on. My stomach turns.

'Everyone ready?' I shout.

'All on board!' replies Bryn.

I push the front of the boat away from the bank with my foot.

I glance down the towpath and to my horror see a shadowy figure running towards us, carrying a torch. It's the burglar and he's catching up quickly.

'Come on!' says Aria. 'Quickly, jump!'

I leap on to the back of the boat as it glides away from the bank. Holding on to the railings that hug the roof, I sidestep along the gunwales on the outside of the boat, back to the cockpit with everyone. I switch the front headlamp on and put the boat in forward.

And then we are driving through the night, the boat chugging onwards.

You're not supposed to run your engines past eight o'clock at night because they can be very loud and disturb neighbours and animals. But this is an emergency.

I watch the kidnapper disappear as we turn a corner.

'He'll catch us, won't he?' asks Keaton, his voice worried and quiet.

'He can't reach us if we're on the boat,' I reply.

Bryn rushes out to join us. 'The safe's gone. And our passports, maybe other stuff too.'

'What are we going to do?' asks Aria, head in hands.

I don't know what to say. It's too much to be in charge all of the time, especially when everything's going so wrong.

All I want is to make everything right again.

Keaton sits on the floor, hunched over his knees.

'Are you OK?' I ask.

What did that man want?' he asks. 'Why did he kidnap you?'

'He wants an old safe we found in the canal,' I explain. 'And he wants it badly enough to ransack our boat for it.'

He groans and slumps over even further. 'How did I get mixed up in this?' he mutters. 'I wish I never came with you. My parents are going to kill me.'

'Hey,' I say, kneeling in front of him. 'It's going to be fine. We can explain everything to your parents in the morning. We can even pull over and let you off now if you want.'

But as I say the words I realise we can't leave him out there in the dark by himself. His eyes are big and glazed over, almost as if he's not there. It reminds me of the times I zone out and think of jellyfish.

'But you're safe here. Don't worry.'

He nods.

My words seem to have calmed him down a bit, for now at least.

Up ahead I see Jenny and Raj's boat. I slow *Newt* as we approach.

'They'll help us,' I say with relief. 'They can call the police.'

I put the boat in reverse as we pull us next to them, to bring her to a stop. *Newt*, like all narrowboats, doesn't have a brake.

'Can you reach their boat?' I ask Aria, moving the tiller back and forth to manoeuvre as close to it as possible.

'I've got it!' says Aria as she steps from *Newt* to the other boat, almost ending up in the splits for a moment. She bangs on the side of their boat.

'Jenny,' she calls. 'Raj! It's Aria.'

There's no sign of movement from inside the boat, no lights coming on. Through the windows everything is dark.

'Try the other end!' I shout.

Aria moves to the back of their boat and knocks against the door. 'Anyone here?' She knocks again, her shouts getting louder and higher in pitch until she's almost crying, banging against the wood with both fists.

I rub my forehead, my stomach sinking. They're not there. No one could sleep through this amount of noise. And their boat is rocking from the waves *Newt*'s creating, along with Aria's weight on the side of the boat. They'd be able to feel it.

'Come back!' I say, worrying about the kidnapper catching up to us.

'Wait!' says Aria. 'I can see Mum's bag.'

'Where?' asks Bryn, shouting across.

'In their porch.'

'Can you get inside?' I ask.

Jenny and Raj's porch is enclosed by a canvas cover, the zip padlocked closed. Aria reaches underneath it and undoes some of the attachments. She crawls underneath.

'There's a bunch of our things here!' she shouts.

'They must have been keeping them for us while the firefighters aired out *Newt*,' I say.

'The safe's here too!' says Aria.

Keaton and I glance at each other. I'm not sure if I want the safe back on our boat. It feels dangerous now.

The logical side of my brain kicks in and I decide that it will be better to have it with us. At least we'll be able to give the safe to the kidnapper if he finds us. Maybe then he'll leave us alone.

'Pass it over!' says Bryn, making his way to the edge of *Newt* and reaching across. Enzo joins him and we do our usual assembly-line technique to pass things on and off the boat.

'Look!' shouts Keaton, pointing behind us. 'He's coming.'

Torchlight bobs along the dark towpath towards us.

'Get back here!' I shout to Aria. 'Quickly.'

Enzo drops the safe and Mum's bag next to the tiller, and he and Bryn reach over to help Aria back on.

I turn the engine to full throttle. Water churns at the sides of the boat. Too late I realise we're heading straight for Jenny and Raj's boat. I slam the tiller in the other direction but it's not turning fast enough – we're going to crash.

Just in time, Enzo reaches for the long stick we use as a punt and presses it against Raj's boat to prevent the collision. He pushes against it, directing *Newt* back out into the canal and I breathe a sigh of relief.

I put *Newt* at maximum speed, even though we're not supposed to go this fast. It creates a wave that washes up against the banks, disturbing the sleeping ducks. Usually I hate it when people speed past; it makes our boat bump into the bank and sometimes things fall off the shelves if it rocks really badly.

'Faster,' says Keaton. 'He's still behind us.'

'I'm going as fast as I can,' I reply. We must be travelling at five or six miles an hour, when usually we only go two and half.

Panic fills my chest.

What do we do if the kidnapper catches us?

I wish that Mum was here. Or Dad.

How am I going to protect everyone by myself?

When Gwyon returned, the sorceress
said only two words.

'About time.'

She plucked the leaf from Gwyon's fingers and
sprinkled it into her pot. The potion bubbled
and swirled in thick shades of brown.

The sorceress told Gwyon the fourth ingredient
to save her brother: a sprig of mugwort.

Chapter Twenty

Kidnapper

Up ahead the canal thins. I realise we're already at the aqueduct, the narrowest part of the whole canal. We'll have to pull the fenders up to fit through. And we're hurtling towards it at full speed.

I jam the boat into reverse to slow us down. We can't enter the narrow aqueduct at this speed. We'll collide against the sides. And there's no way I want anything else to happen to poor *Newt*. She's been through enough already.

Aria is already climbing all over the boat, pulling up the fenders.

'It's so we can fit through the aqueduct,' I explain to Keaton.

'What's an aqueduct?' asks Keaton.

'It carries the canal over the River Avon.'

'It's amazing,' says Bryn. 'It's a hundred and fifty foot high.'

Keaton's eyes widen. 'That high?'

'Yeah,' says Bryn. 'And it's one of the only places where a canal crosses a river.'

'Water on water,' says Aria.

'What if we fall off?' asks Keaton.

'Be quiet,' I say, exasperated. 'I need to concentrate.'

I've finally managed to slow down *Newt* enough. I line her up carefully with the entrance, making sure we're straight.

'Is this it?' asks Keaton, as we enter. He grips on to the railing next to him.

Enzo opens his notebook and scribbles some words: 'Are you afraid of heights?'

Keaton nods. 'I'm *very* afraid of heights.'

'I can hold your hand if you want,' says Aria.

'Thanks,' he said, giving her a faint grin. 'But I think I'm just going to shut my eyes.'

We enter the narrow aqueduct. On a clear day you can see for miles from up here. Below us I can hear the raging river.

'You have to look,' says Aria, tapping Keaton's arm. He has his eyes shut tight. 'It's pretty! You can see the moon reflecting in the river.'

Keaton opens one eye a tiny slit. 'I've never been this high up.' He squeezes it closed again.

'We're off now,' I say, moments later. 'It's over.' I smile; I didn't even bump into the side once. Mum would be proud.

'Should we stop and get help?' asks Bryn.

I glance behind us. I can't see the bob of the kidnapper's torch. We've managed to put some distance between him and us; we'll have time to slow down and ask for help. But I realise there are hardly any boats from this point on and all the ones we pass are empty. We're entering winter and this section of the canal clears then as many of the boats move to the marinas.

'Do you think the kidnapper can still see us?' asks Aria, turning back and looking over her shoulder.

'He might be able to see our headlamp,' I reply.

'Can we turn the light off then?' she asks.

I hesitate. 'We can try,' I say at last. 'But I might need it to steer.'

I switch the light off and we're immediately plunged into darkness. Above us, clouds pass in front of the moon. I listen to the rhythm of the engine. Usually it would lull me to sleep but tonight I'm alert, more alert than I've ever been. I struggle to see without the front light. I try and focus on the silver ripples of moonlight reflecting on the water and travelling in a straight line.

But it's too hard to judge the bends ahead and we almost crash into the bank.

The boat wobbles from side to side.

I shake my head, exasperated. 'I need the light.'

Aria switches it back on reluctantly.

'Why do you think the kidnapper wants this stupid safe so badly?' I ask. With one hand I reach and shake it, half expecting it to pop open.

Enzo shivers. None of us are dressed properly for a night out on the boat.

'Here,' I say to Keaton. 'Take the tiller for a second. I want to get a blanket.'

Bryn and Aria are staring out the back, keeping an eye out for the kidnapper.

Keaton frowns. 'I don't know how to steer a boat.'

'It's easy,' I say. 'Just hold the tiller straight. If you want *Newt* to go to the left, you push the tiller to the right, and vice versa.'

'What if I crash?'

'You won't,' I say. 'You've got this.'

'I'll steer,' says Enzo, rolling his eyes at Keaton and taking the tiller.

'Thanks,' says Keaton, sitting back down.

I enter the kitchen through the hatch at the back of the boat. The first thing that hits me is the smell. It still stinks of smoke so strongly I can taste it in the back of my mouth and it stings my nostrils.

The ceiling in the living room is charred black in places. The cement is cracked and chipped where the flue pipe joins the wood-burner. The firefighter said that's how the fire started, spreading from our wood-burner. I shake my head at it. We had it checked last year.

I quickly pass and stop in my bedroom nook. Everything's been turned upside down. On the floor is the compass Dad gave me, a birthday gift so that I would always be able to tell which direction Wales was in from the canal in England. I lift it over my head, wearing it like a necklace. It's cold against my skin but I like the way the weight of it feels.

I take a blanket from Mum's bed. Her room is the one furthest away from the fire, so I'm hoping the stuff in it will smell the least. I press the blanket against my cheek. It still smells faintly of her coconut moisturiser.

It all comes back then. The secret I've been carrying all this time about the night she fell.

One I can't even allow myself to remember, let alone say out aloud. Because saying it will make it true. And if it is true, then it's the worst thing I've ever done. It will mean that all of this is my fault.

My breath catches and I run out of Mum's room to escape my thoughts. I reach the deck and double over, breathing quickly. I gulp down the cool fresh air. Collecting myself, I wipe my eyes and return to everyone. They huddle under the blanket.

The sky is transforming from black into deep shades of blue as the sun rises. A robin sings in the hedgerow next to us. Frosty spider's webs decorate the branches alongside the canal. Beyond, fields stretch on either side, filled with baaing sheep. Fog rolls across the surface of the water and over the fields.

We're no longer hidden by the darkness and I glance behind us, searching for signs of the kidnapper.

'Red sky in the morning,' says Aria as a thin

strip of pink appears on the horizon, 'shepherd's warning.'

I shiver. There are many things we could be being warned about right now.

'Mum would love this morning,' says Aria. 'You can hear a fieldfare thrush chattering. Listen.'

'We can tell her about it soon,' I say.

'I'm hungry,' says Aria, rubbing her tummy.

'Why don't you and Bryn get some food from the kitchen and bring it up to the cockpit,' I say.

They disappear and return with Mum's homemade jams and crackers, a packet of chocolate biscuits, a bag of dates, baked beans, a tin opener and dog food for Willow.

'I had to wash the plates,' says Aria, handing them out. 'They were covered in ash and soot.'

We've been on a straight section of canal for a while. I glance behind me and my shoulders tighten.

Unbelievably, a torch beam bobs in the distance.

Aria follows my line of sight. 'The kidnapper!' she shouts. 'Look, he's still following us.'

Aria, Bryn and Keaton rush to the back to get a better look.

'What are we going to do?' asks Enzo.

'I don't know,' I say, shaking my head.

The things I do know are: One, we can easily

be followed in the boat. Two, there are no other boats on the canal here and no one to help us. Three, we'll run out of diesel soon.

And then I realise a fourth thing. Ahead is a flight of locks that lead the canal into the city of Bath and then the River Avon. The river currents are too strong at this time of year for us to navigate them. We'll get washed away if we try. There's not even enough time for us to open and close the lock gates to get there.

Soon we'll have no choice but to pull over.

Exhausted, Gwyon lay down on her bed of moss.
She hadn't slept more than a few hours since
she started the search for the ingredients.

But the sorceress woke her up moments later.

'The ingredients are complete. But now the hard work
must begin. You need to watch that potion for three
months. Keep stirring it. And make sure that the fire
never goes out. After that, I promise you I'll give you
the last ingredient and the recipe to cure your brother.'

Gwyon thought that this would be the last potion
she ever made for the sorceress. And everything
would be worth it if she could save her brother.

Chapter Twenty-One
Journey

I picture Bath, the city ahead of us. Sometimes we moor there in summer to buy clothes, visit the parks or to see a play. I try and remember if I've seen a police station there but I have no idea where it might be.

Where else could we go?

I glance behind us. The torchlight has gone, but I know he must still be out there. I have an idea. It's risky but I can't see any other option.

'Listen,' I say to everyone. They turn, looking up at me with tired eyes. 'We're going to have to stop soon.'

'Why?' asks Aria. 'I don't want to get off the boat.'

'Yeah, we're safe on here,' says Bryn, crossing his arms.

'We have to. We're coming up to the locks,' I say.

Bryn, Enzo and Aria look at each other with worried faces. Keaton looks confused.

'But I have a plan,' I continue. 'We can go to the train station in Bath. It's close to the locks and the canal. We should be able to outrun the kidnapper. And once we're safely on the train, we can get help. What do you think?'

'We'll have to outrun him all the way to the station,' says Keaton. 'Even if it's just a few minutes, that'll be tricky.'

'He's probably tired,' says Aria. 'He's been on foot this whole time. So we have an advantage.'

'Do you know the way?' Keaton asks me.

I nod. 'I've done the walk from the canal to the train station hundreds of times.'

'OK,' says Keaton at last. 'I trust you.'

'Everyone agree with the plan?' I ask.

Everyone nods. Bryn rubs his lip. 'I still wish we could stay on *Newt*.'

'Can you steer for a minute?' I ask Enzo.

I dart into the cabins and grab my survival book. I open it and flick through. It doesn't say anything about how to deal with kidnappers and burglars. It's more about how to survive in the wilderness.

I stop at the page that says survival kit supplies. I gather the items I can find:

Sleeping Bag

Check. I remember how cold it was at Keaton's and grab four, shoving three in a separate backpack for Enzo to carry. We were all given them last year for Christmas; they're extra-warm ones. They'll be useful if we have to go back Keaton's.

Warm Clothes

Check. I pile everyone's coats over my arm, even though they smell terrible, like burnt hair.

Matches

Check. The ones by the fireplace must have gone up in flames but the spare packet in the kitchen is still intact.

Flint

Nope. I don't think I've ever even seen flint before. I'm sure we'll be fine without it but I grab some newspaper instead.

Magnifying Glass

I remember that Aria was using one to examine the moss and find it in the bathroom.

Rope

Check. We always have spare rope on the boat.

Needle and Thread

Check. Mum keeps some in our bits and pieces drawer.

Compass

Check. It's around my neck. I close my palm around it.

Medical Kit

Check. We have one in the kitchen.

Signal Flares

Definitely not.

Torch

Check.

Water

Check. I fill a bottle in the sink and shove it into my now-heavy backpack.

Penknife

Check. I remember seeing one in the medical kit.

Food

Check. I grab a jar of dried dog food to bring with us and stuff it into the bag with some more of Mum's jams, peanut butter, a whole loaf of bread I find in the fridge, and packets of biscuits. We're going to need snacks if we have to stay at Keaton's again. I'm still barefoot, so I also grab an old pair of trainers and slip them on.

Now I feel prepared.

I leave the windows open a crack to air *Newt* out. I drape a blanket over the broken window to try and disguise it. Pausing before I return to the cockpit, I run back to Mum's room, grabbing some things I think she'd like to have in the hospital with her: a picture of us all she keeps by her bed, her lucky piece of rose quartz and a small teddy bear she's had since she was a child.

'Cara!' Bryn shouts at me. 'It's time to moor.'

I heft my backpack on to my shoulders and dash on to the deck. I hand out everyone's coats and a blanket for Keaton. We don't have any coats big enough for him.

'Hurry up,' shouts Aria. 'What on earth is in there?' she asks when she sees my overstuffed backpack.

'Things for Mum,' I say.

Glancing along the towpath to check our pursuer isn't there, I take the tiller and direct *Newt* over to the side. Aria and Bryn jump off as I approach the bank and tug the boat in by its ropes. They hammer the mooring pins into the ground.

I switch off the engine and jump ashore, helping them with the pins. Willow leaps off the boat on to the bank and sniffs around the tufts of grass at the side of the towpath. It's early morning now and a daytime moon hangs in the sky. Enzo jumps on to the path behind Willow, followed by Keaton who carefully clambers over the side.

Bryn carries the safe by its handle.

As we leave, I turn to *Newt*. 'Be safe,' I whisper. She looks sad with her smashed window and empty of people. 'We'll be back soon.'

December 16th – Present Day

Just before we left, I turned to look behind me. And I saw something that made my heart stop. Our pursuer was still behind us - I could see a torch bobbing faintly through the trees. And that's when I realised; he wasn't on foot. He must have found a bike. And that meant that he could catch up to us.

After two and a half months of Gwyon stirring, the sorceress checked on the potion and pressed her palms together with excitement.

'It's almost ready. Soon all the knowledge in the world will be mine,' said the sorceress, as she stared into the potion she'd created. 'By the time it's ready, it will be concentrated into a single drop. A single drop of knowledge. Of power.'

Chapter Twenty-Two
Countryside

'He has a bike. Everyone, run!' I shout. 'Quickly, follow me!'

Keaton opens his mouth but I interrupt him. 'There's no time for questions.' I take Bryn and Aria's hands and start sprinting.

Enzo, Keaton and Willow take off after me in a thunder of steady thudding as our feet hit the gravelly towpath. We run as fast as we can past the gardens on either side of us, no longer in the countryside but in the city. Georgian stone houses stand on either side of the towpath. In the distance is the top of a church spire.

Soon, I duck off the towpath and along the streets. This route will be quicker. And maybe the kidnapper won't notice which way we went.

Minutes later, we enter the back entrance to the train station, the same way we always come with Mum. The barriers are open and I usher everyone up the stairs. I can see on the boards that a train is coming into platform 2, so I lead us towards it.

There is a crowd of people standing on the platform, dressed smartly in winter coats, drinking coffee, or staring at their phones. Pigeons strut back and forth between them.

I wait impatiently. Then I spot something that sends fear shooting through my body.

A man coming up the stairs behind us in a big overcoat.

A flash of green scarf.

The train is pulling into the platform.

'Follow me,' I hiss. He hasn't seen us yet — I can see him craning his neck to search through the crowd.

As the train stops, I push to the front of the queue. People move out of the way for Willow.

We hop aboard and hurry to the carriage at the back of the train.

The only thought flashing through my head is to get us as far away from the kidnapper as possible.

'Where's this train going?' asks Bryn.

I quickly glance up at the board.

'Newport.'

I hold my breath as the last person gets on, trying to see whether our kidnapper is still on the platform. I can't see anything.

Just as the train doors beep and close, I catch sight of him frantically scanning the platform and the train, looking for us. The train pulls away, leaving him behind, and I take a deep breath.

We find a table of four and sit down, the twins squishing into one seat. Bryn is still clutching the safe on his lap.

'What are we going to do in Newport?' asks Bryn.

'It's halfway to Dad's,' I say, suddenly realising. 'We could go and find him.'

'I don't know about this,' says Keaton.

'You can go home if you want,' I say, snapping at him, tired of his worries. 'Get off at the next stop. I've got enough to deal with as it is.'

'I kind of feel like we're in this together now,' whispers Keaton. 'I just know that my parents will be worrying about me soon.'

I feel myself calm. He has a point. 'I understand.'

'Do you even know how to get all the way to Dad's?' asks Aria.

'Of course,' I reply, trying to tame my shaky voice and sound confident. 'We've done it loads of times, haven't we? We change trains in Newport for Fishguard, then from the train station it's only a short drive into the woods to Dad's cabin. We'll have to walk that part but it's not far.'

'Will Dad be back from his research trip?' asks Enzo.

I work out what day it is in my head. Today is Thursday. 'He'll be back tonight!' I say. 'It's perfect!'

My body aches with tiredness. The idea of finding Dad and letting him deal with everything that's happened sounds so appealing.

Keaton shakes his head. 'We should just tell the police what happened.'

'We could,' I say. 'We could tell them how we were out in the middle of the night stealing our dog back from a shelter, when we were kidnapped by a burglar, before escaping on a boat.'

'No one's going to believe that,' says Aria. 'Unless we see the kidnapper again.' She lifts her chin. 'And if we do, then I'm going to scream as loudly as I can.'

'OK, OK. Point taken,' says Keaton. 'How long do you think it will take to get to your dad's cabin?'

'We'll be there by the afternoon,' I say.

'I think it's a good plan,' says Enzo.

'I guess that works,' says Keaton.

I stare outside at the misty fields speeding by, wondering whether or not we are doing the right thing.

After an hour of worrying, it's time to change trains. People usually make room for us with Willow because she's so big but it's morning rush hour and the next train is packed. I have to stand up by the door, holding Willow close to me. I lean against the wall, thankful to be on our way to see Dad.

I just hope the kidnapper didn't follow us.

After a few stops the train empties and we squeeze on to some seats around a table. Willow lies on the row behind us, happy to rest her head on her legs.

I rest my head back against the seat and close my eyes, drifting in and out of sleep.

After a while, Bryn grabs my arm. 'The conductor's coming,' he whispers.

Keaton stiffens. 'We haven't got a ticket, have we?'

'What should we do?' asks Aria, nervously kicking her legs back and forth under the seat.

'Shh,' I say.

We can't get caught now.

I dig around in the backpack as the conductor approaches, pretending to search for the tickets. He watches as I open flaps and undo zips.

'I think I lost our tickets,' I say at last.

'They might have fallen out of our pockets when we were skipping,' says Aria.

I widen my eyes at Aria, urging her to stay quiet. Now is not the time for her imaginative stories. The conductor doesn't need to know how we lost the tickets.

'I'm sorry,' I say. 'Our dad's collecting us at the station. He can give you some more money to pay for the tickets.'

'Your dad's meeting you?' asks the conductor.

We all nod and smile.

'Shouldn't you be in school?' the conductor asks slowly, and I realise since it's Thursday everyone else will be in school.

'We're home-schooled,' says Keaton.

'All right. Just this once,' the conductor says, printing some tickets out for us.

'Thanks,' I say, relief rushing over me.

The train whizzes through the countryside, taking us further and further away from the cities and deeper and deeper into the wilderness. We doze a bit, but time passes very slowly.

'I am so bored,' says Aria, folding her arms. 'I feel like we've been on this train for hours and hours and hours.'

'We have,' says Enzo.

Bryn has his ear to the safe and is moving the numbers of the lock. 'I need a stethoscope,' he says.

'Why?' I ask.

'I just remembered that ages ago we watched a film about bank robbers and that was how they got into the safe with the diamonds. With a stethoscope.'

'Just leave the safe alone right now,' I say, glancing around me uneasily. 'Someone might see us. Pretend we're on an undercover mission.'

'What film was it?' asks Keaton.

'Some cartoon,' says Bryn. 'I can't remember the name of it.'

I think about Keaton's house and realise I don't remember seeing a TV.

'You probably wouldn't know it,' I say. In my tiredness, the words come out sounding harsher than I mean them to.

'Did I do something to upset you?' asks Keaton. 'I feel like you've had it in for me before you even came to my house.'

I remember the sniggering at the back of the class. The text messages flash into my mind. My face burns.

'You laughed at my talk. You obviously thought it was stupid.'

'I have no idea what you're talking about,' replies Keaton, looking bewildered.

'You don't?' I ask again.

He shakes his head. 'I wasn't laughing. And I didn't think your talk was stupid.'

I examine his face for signs he's lying. His eyes meet mine steadily.

'OK,' I say and smile at him. It feels nice not to be suspicious of him any more.

The train slows and I look up at the screen.

'This is our stop,' I say.

'Yes!' says Bryn, jumping up. 'Finally.'

Enzo fetches Willow, Bryn takes his safe, and Keaton takes Aria's hand. We make our way through the carriage to the door.

Willow wags her tail as we open the door window and watch the train chug into the tiny platform.

I can't shake the feeling that we're still being followed and just in case, I usher everyone off the train and we hide behind a ticket machine that says *out of order*. Watching the other passengers disembark, I study them for a green scarf or big coat. I see nothing worrying; just an ordinary crowd of commuters hurrying to work.

I lean back against the wall.

I think we're finally safe.

December 16th – Present Day

Looking back, I probably should have told someone about the kidnapper then. But I really didn't think anybody would believe me. Would you?

Gwyon realised then that the potion could be dangerous; it was far too strong for one person. But she only had two more weeks to wait before she could save her brother. She pushed her worry aside and stirred the pot and the potion grew thicker, and she counted down the days until she could finally stop working for the sorceress. Every evening she took charcoal from the fire and used it to mark another day off on the wall of the cave.

Chapter Twenty-Three
Seashell

Dad lives in a cabin in the Pembrokeshire Coast National Park, in the Preseli Mountains. The landscape here is different to our flat canal, more dramatic. Around us are rugged cliffs and fields dotted with stone farmhouses.

'We must be near the sea!' says Aria.

'I smell it!' says Bryn.

'I see it!' says Aria.

Straight ahead of us a road winds down to rocks and a golden beach.

'I'm going in!' shrieks Aria.

'If you're going in then I'm going in too,' calls Bryn.

Bryn passes me the safe and they both gallop off towards the beach without a glance backwards.

'Stop!' I shout. 'We don't have time!'

Enzo raises an eyebrow at me. 'What did you expect?'

Willow whines and Enzo nods his head, giving her permission to dash after them, which she does, kicking up sand behind her.

Keaton, Enzo and I follow. There are a few people on the beach. The air is fresh and salty. I recognise the area, I realise. We drove past it last month with Dad. We're close to his cabin. I glance at the sun anxiously. I want to get to the cabin before dark. The trains usually take about five hours and we got on the 07.32 this morning, which means it's almost one in the afternoon.

The twins are rolling up their trousers and wading into the waves.

'Five minutes!' I call to them. 'Then we have to get going.'

The sand gets in my socks and I take off my shoes, hopping on one foot.

Willow bounds out of the water and shakes her coat, spraying water droplets all over me.

'Come on,' I shout, standing at the edge of the sea. Each retreating wave reveals shiny stones, smooth glass and seashells.

The wind whooshes past my ears. Seagulls squawk and gather around a man eating crisps.

'Just one more minute,' says Aria. 'You should all come in!'

'Is it warm?' asks Keaton, cautiously.

Enzo shakes his head but gestures at Keaton to follow him in. 'It's not too bad.'

They remove their socks and shoes. Keaton rolls his trousers up as high as they'll go and dips his toes in. He shrieks and laughs.

Aria giggles. 'Told you it was fun!'

The sun glitters on the water's surface. Growing up on water I feel at home by it. I'm tired and stiff. I put my feet in the waves and splash some more on my face. It runs down my head and the back of my neck, waking me up.

I glance again at the sun. Time to go.

'Everyone out!' I yell, copying Mum's firm voice.

And this time everyone listens. With no towels to dry their legs, Aria and Bryn jump up and down, shaking the water off like Willow. Bryn enters wild mode and runs around spinning and leaping and roaring at the top of his voice with Willow chasing him.

The wind howls around us. I shiver. Willow digs a hole with her large paws.

'Look what I found,' says Aria, holding out her hand. In her palm is a drill-shaped shell.

'You can show Dad when we find him,' I say.

'If you hold it under the water it sparkles,' she says.

Once we're all sort of dry and have our shoes back on, I head towards the road.

'So do you know the way?' asks Enzo.

'Yeah. We walk along the beach and then there's a road that leads from here towards Dad's cabin. We just need to follow it,' I say.

I get the compass out and line up the arrow with the direction of north. 'We have to head north east when we reach the road.' I set the direction to NE and then spin the compass around so that the red line that always points to the north pole is lined up with the north arrow on the compass. I remember Dad using his cabin as an example when he taught me how to use the compass.

As I fiddle with the compass and Enzo tosses sticks for Willow, Keaton and the twins take it in turns spinning the dial of the safe. 'Do you think we'll ever get it open?' asks Aria.

'We have to,' says Bryn. 'Now we have proof there's something incredible inside.'

Keaton nods. 'You're right. Why else would that man want it so badly?'

'Maybe we should tell the police and they can open it for us,' suggests Aria.

'Come on,' I say, satisfied I know the right direction. 'It's this way.'

We walk along the beach to get to the road. Bryn drags behind and Keaton carries the safe for him.

'Do you remember when Dad took us to Borth Beach?' I ask, thinking that it must be just one or two beaches over.

Bryn thinks. 'Is that the one with the underwater forest?' he asks.

I nod. When the tide is out, a submerged forest appears from under the sea. Dad grew up near there and he couldn't wait to show it to us, but when we got there the tide was in and we had to wait for hours and hours for it to go out. It was worth it to see the lost land of petrified tree stumps though.

I look out to sea and wonder if there's anything hidden under these waves. I spot a seal sunbathing on a rock. Aria sees it too.

'A seal!' she says. 'Or maybe it's a mermaid in disguise.'

I laugh. We're nearly at the road. We clamber over the rocks to get there. A seagull swoops low above my head and I flinch. Even though I think we lost the kidnapper, I still feel on edge, as if he could show back up at any moment and ruin everything.

One evening, Gwyon accidentally stepped on the pile of wood and kindling for the fire and a holly leaf and pricked her toes. She hopped on one foot, yelping in pain. And as she did, she bumped into the pot holding the potion.

Chapter Twenty-Four
Accident

'See that arch?' says Aria, pointing to a huge rock jutting out of the waves in the distance. The crashing waves have worn away part of the rock and there's a tunnel going through it.

We all nod.

'That's the door to the mermaid kingdom,' says Aria. 'You just have to swim through.'

'*I* think that's where the sharks live,' says Bryn.

'Mermaids have pet sharks,' says Aria.

Enzo stops. He crouches down and stares at something in the rocks.

'A rock pool,' he says. 'There's a crab.'

We all crouch around it and watch the crab sidestep and hide under a rock, one pincer sticking out.

'Come on,' I say. 'Let's stay focused. It'll just be a few hours now.'

But I watch the crab for a few more moments. After the stress of the last few days it's nice to pretend everything's normal. Even just for a second.

I look at Keaton's excited face as he watches the crab and wonder how many times he's done something like this.

'Is she always like that, your mum?' I ask.

'Like what?' asks Keaton.

'Strict.'

'I suppose,' he says. 'She just worries a lot.'

We stand and start to walk on again.

'I'm just glad you're not allergic to Willow,' says Aria, taking Keaton's hand and skipping alongside him.

'Me too,' says Keaton.

We leave the beach and step on to the road. It's narrow with thick woodland on either side of it.

'Single file,' I say. 'There's no pavement.'

We walk for about an hour. Aria's feet drag.

The word 'Araf', which means slow in Welsh, is painted on the tarmac.

We couldn't possibly go any slower.

Soon Bryn starts to whine.

'Are we there yet?' he asks.

'Just a bit further,' I say.

'Let's play I spy,' says Aria, which is what Mum plays with us on long car journeys. 'I'll start. I spy with my little eye, something the colour green.'

'A tree,' says Bryn.

'A bird,' says Keaton.

'My jumper!' says Enzo.

'Enzo's right. It was his jumper.'

'Do you hear that?' I ask. 'I think there's a car coming. Everyone on to the grassy verge.'

'Ouch!' shouts Aria from behind me. 'Cara!'

I spin around and see her losing her balance, tumbling backwards down a steep slope into the woods. I run after her, skidding on loose leaves and grabbing on to trunks to steady myself. She rolls backwards until she reaches the bottom.

'Aria!' I call. 'Are you all right?'

I reach her.

She lifts up her palms and says, 'Stinging nettles.' Her bottom lip sticks out.

'Are you hurt anywhere else?'

She shakes her head. I look up the slope and see Keaton and Bryn sliding down on their bums, followed by Enzo scrambling down with Willow.

'Let's find a dock leaf.' They usually grow near stinging nettles. I search the area for the broad leaves. Then I hear the rush of water and realise there's a river gushing past.

'Why don't you rinse your hands in the water,' I say. 'It might help.'

She nods and I help her over to the water's edge.

The others catch up to us.

'It smells like flowers around here,' says Aria.

'I'm starving,' says Enzo.

'Me too,' says Bryn.

'Here,' I say, opening a pack of biscuits and offering them round.

'Not fair,' says Bryn. 'Aria took two.'

'Telltale,' says Aria, sticking her tongue out at him. 'I was going to share it with you.'

'There's a whole packet here, don't worry,' I say.

But a whole packet between five only comes to two and a half each and I'm left wondering if I brought enough food. I try to shake the worry; we'll be at Dad's in a few hours.

Enzo takes out the jar of Willow's food and tips some on a rock for her.

Bryn lifts a log up revealing a whole habitat of invertebrates underneath; woodlice crawl over worms, and a snail sticks to the underside of the wood.

Willow dives into the river and frolics, jumping over the currents. When she finally gets out she shakes out her coat, spraying droplets everywhere.

Then she barks. She's found something. I look closer. An otter with greyish-brown fur and a cream-coloured chest and throat pops its head out of a burrow at the side of the bank.

'Look, everyone,' I whisper, raising a finger to my lips.

The otter swims into the river with her webbed feet, paddling forwards. Behind her follow three otter pups. They twist and turn in the water playing.

Willow wags her tail in excitement and leaps into the water with them.

I expect the otters to scarper but instead they play tag with her, swimming in and out of her legs and around her in circles. One of the otter pups floats on its back and rubs its tummy, grooming itself.

'Can we swim with them?' asks Aria, bouncing up and down on her toes. 'Please?'

A part of me is too tired to argue.

'Just quickly,' I say.

Aria and Bryn pull off their jumpers and trousers and wade into the river, splashing and chasing the otters.

The otters scarper. I watch them playing together and decide that the water might wake me up. I strip down to my underwear before plunging my whole body in for a second. It's freezing and takes my breath away. I tread water to warm up. Then I float on my back and look up at the sky, feeling the sun on my skin through the trees. I remember that everyone else is in school today and wonder if they're worrying about us being missing. I close my eyes; I've felt heavy ever since I started school, like there's a weight pushing me down and I just want to feel light for a second.

The current crashes over me.

'Help!' shouts Bryn.

His voice is sharp and worried.

I'm upright immediately, looking around.

It takes me a second to register what's happened.

'Aria!' screams Keaton.

She's in the water and she's swam too far out; she's being pulled downstream by the strong current.

I wade to the bank as fast as I can and run along the edge of the river after her. Her head bobs under water and then comes back up. She thrashes in the current.

I don't know if I'm a strong enough swimmer to go in after her. I could get washed away by the rapids too.

My heart races. I leap on to a rock to get closer, slipping on moss. I'm still too far away to grab Aria.

What do I do?

Gwyon stumbled and crashed into the pot. The pot tipped and potion flew into the air in droplets. Several landed on the side of Gwyon's hand. They burnt her and she immediately sucked her skin to numb the pain.

When she looked up, the sorceress loomed over her, desperate and furious.

Chapter Twenty-Five
Hazelnut

Willow gallops past me, knocking me off my feet and leaping into the river off a ridge. She paddles towards Aria.

Mum, slipping from the plank and into the canal.

I run after them along the bank.

'Aria!' cries Bryn from shore.

Willow reaches Aria and uses her nose to lift her slightly and push her towards the bank. But the current is strong and they're both still being carried downriver.

I scramble down the bank and wade into the water to meet them, holding on to an overhanging branch to steady myself and prevent being swept away too. Keaton and Enzo join me.

'Come on, Willow!' I shout.

Keaton wraps his arm around a branch, Enzo holds his other hand and I take his, so that I can reach further out. Willow paddles onwards and I stretch out as far as I can, my hand clinging to Enzo's, until I can just reach Aria with my fingertips. I grab her soaked vest and pull it towards me. Then she's close enough for me to reach her hands and I grip them tightly. Enzo and Keaton help me lift her out. Bryn is further up on the bank, pale and frightened-looking.

'Aria?' I say, pushing her hair out of her face and patting her back. My fingernails have left crescent moons imprinted in her skin. She coughs and splutters. Opening her eyes, she gazes up at us. She's awake.

Willow pants beside us. Enzo strokes her back and rests his head against hers.

'Does anywhere hurt?' I ask.

'Just my chest,' she replies, and coughs again.

Keaton takes off his jumper and we rub her as dry as we can, then tug it over her head.

I can tell she's in shock. Willow lies over Aria's legs, using her own body heat to warm Aria and I rub her arms and chest to get the blood moving.

After a few minutes I ask Aria, 'Are you feeling any better?'

She nods. 'I swallowed some water and it went down the wrong way but I think I've coughed it all up now.'

I stroke her wet hair, thankful she's OK. I rest my forehead against Willow's head and whisper, 'What would we do without you?'

I fetch my clothes and dress with shaky hands. They're covered in mud and I wipe them on my trousers.

We all lie on the ground next to Aria, looking up at the trees and their leaves. I take a breath, in and out.

'Did you ever notice the ways the trees don't touch each other?' asks Bryn.

'Oh yeah,' I say. 'It's called "crown shyness".'

'It looks like a green jigsaw puzzle,' says Bryn, turning his head to the side.

'It's so they can all get enough light,' I say.

'It's getting late,' says Keaton quietly.

He's right. The sun is already low in the sky. I think it's about two or three o'clock by now.

'Can you stand?' I ask Aria.

She nods and we slowly help her up.

'I can give you a piggyback for a while?' suggests Keaton.

Aria smiles and nods. We all start walking again. I stare up at the sky through the dappled tree light. We only have a few hours of daylight left and not much food, only some bread, jam and peanut butter.

Why did I let them swim?

As I'm staring up at the branches, I notice something else: brown, round hazelnuts growing amongst the leaves. I gaze deeper into the branches; most of the nuts are still green and not yet mature enough to eat but there are definitely some brown ones too. I reach up and pick one. I pull the papery husk off before putting it on a rock and giving it a sharp tap with a stone. The shell cracks first time.

'Anyone want one?' I ask, holding it out.

Keaton eyes the hazelnut sceptically. 'I'm not eating that. How do you know it's edible?'

'It's a hazelnut!' I say.

'I'll go first.' I bite the nut in half. I offer him the other half, but he waits until I crunch and swallow and then a few more seconds to check that nothing bad happens to me before he wipes his half on his T-shirt and nibbles on the edge.

'Not bad,' he says.

I smile, glad he decided to try it.

'This one has teeth marks on it!' says Enzo. We gather round and examine it. There's a hole in the shell, with tiny teeth marks bordering it.

'Maybe it was a fairy,' says Aria.

'Probably a mouse,' says Enzo.

'Do you often pick nuts and things?' asks Keaton.

I nod. 'We never collect mushrooms though. It's too hard to tell the deadly ones from the good ones.'

I spot a squirrel watching us from a tree, perched on a branch with furry red ears and clasping an acorn in its claws.

'Don't worry, little one,' I say. 'We'll leave some for you. Is everyone good to keep walking now? We're almost there!'

'And then we'll find Dad,' says Bryn happily, taking my hand. 'And we can call Mum. She'll be better now, won't she?'

I nod. 'She's going to be just fine.'

But I realise that I don't know this for sure. I don't know anything for sure any more.

As Gwyon sucked on her burnt finger she swallowed
a drop of the potion, and in that drop was the
whole universe. The knowledge pulsed through her
veins, all around her body and in that moment, she
knew that the sorceress would never let her live.

The potion was gone. And Gwyon had
accidentally drunk the last drop.

Chapter Twenty-Six
Compass

We walk on. Crispy leaves get caught in my shoelaces. It's hard going.

'I think we should try and get back on the main road,' I say after a while.

We all stop and stare at the steep hill up to the road.

'There might be an easier route up,' says Enzo. 'I'll check.'

Enzo scrambles up, pulling himself up by roots and plants at first. The wind blows his long hair behind him. A few times I see him struggle to keep his footholds on the slippery rocks, but each time I think he might fall, he manages to steady himself and continues climbing up until finally he heaves himself over the ridge. Willow follows him. He looks around, then signs at us, beaming.

'There's an animal path over there. It's less steep.' His hair is windswept.

I usher Keaton, Bryn and Aria in the direction he points in, spotting a thin path winding up the slope. I clamber up the route first, pausing to catch my breath.

'Are you OK?' I ask Enzo when I reach him, looking at his hands. His palms are scratched.

He nods.

And within minutes we're on the road again, back on the right route to the cabin.

Soon, the daylight is fading into blue dusk. The twins are tired and Enzo has dark rings around his eyes. So much has happened since last night and we've travelled so far.

I swat a swarm of midges away from my face.

'Can we take a break?' asks Bryn. He's dragging the safe.

'Just a bit further,' I say, taking the safe from him. I want to keep moving. And even though the kidnapper must be long gone, I still have a sense that we might be being followed, as if he could reappear at any second. I think of Mum and wonder if she's awake now. I wonder whether she knows that we're missing.

As dusk hits, tiny bats flitter in and out of the hedgerows around us, searching for insects.

'I think they're pipistrelles,' Enzo says. He's been fascinated with bats ever since he discovered they use echolocation.

He gasps as he spots a larger bat flying in circles above us. 'It could be a greater horseshoe bat,' he says, smiling. 'They live in this part of Wales.'

I urge him onwards and we continue to follow the road. We're deep in the national park now. There's no one else about.

We turn a corner and I see something that sends a knot to the pit of my stomach. Ahead of us is a mountain. Dad lives on the other side of it. This road winds all the way around. In the car we drive around it in minutes but I realise it might take hours to walk.

How can the journey be so much longer on foot?

I stop in the road and Keaton, who is carrying Aria, bumps into the back of me.

Everyone pauses and follows my line of sight.

'I forgot about Carningli Mountain,' I say.

'Is that the angel mountain?' asks Aria.

I nod.

'It looks like a volcano,' says Keaton.

'It is,' I say. 'An ancient volcano. Dad lives in the forest on the other side of it.'

'I think we should go over the top of it,' says Bryn. 'That will be much quicker than going all the way around. Besides, it's really a hill, not a mountain, right?'

'*How* ancient is this volcano?' asks Keaton.

'I think its last eruption was four hundred and fifty million years ago,' I say. 'So you don't have to worry about that.' He laughs. 'Who thinks we should go over the top of it?'

Everyone raises their hand.

'It's decided,' I say. 'We're heading up.'

We cut up through the fields. Our only company are sheep with thick woolly coats and long tails. In the last of the daylight, the view behind us stretches from fields and hills of green to the brown of the cliffs and the blue of the sea in the distance. Wispy clouds turn pink in the sunset. As we get higher, the terrain gets steeper and we have to scramble up the scree slope.

'My legs hurt!' says Bryn.

'I want to go back to the canal. It's flat, flat, flat,' sings Aria.

'You said we'd be there by now,' says Keaton.

'Well, I'm sorry if I don't know everything,' I snap at him.

I'm trying my best.

My heart pumps hard. I want to keep going but I can see the twins are exhausted though. The sky is darkening fast.

'Let's take a break,' I say, spotting a flat ridge sheltered by stones.

Out of breath, we sit, leaning back against the stones and look out over the view, lit up in dark purples from the sunset. I break up bits of twigs between my fingers. The stones block out the fierce wind.

I reach into the backpack and grab a torch and switch it on, resting it in my lap to make peanut butter sandwiches.

I thought we'd be there hours ago. Bryn yawns.

We're going to have to stop for a while.

Shivering, I undo the sleeping bags from the backpacks. We huddle together and climb inside them. Aria and Bryn share a sleeping bag so that Keaton can have one too.

'I'm too tired to keep walking right now,' says Aria.

I spot some branches lying on the ground ahead.

'I'll make us a fire so that we can warm up before we carry on,' I say.

Luckily it doesn't feel like it's going to rain, so we just have to focus on staying warm.

Enzo helps me gather the sticks and arrange them over the newspaper. I light a match and hold it to the edge of the paper. The flames flicker and catch, shining green and blue from the ink. The wood crackles.

Aria drifts asleep with some of the bread still in her hand. Soon the others have closed their eyes too, resting their heads against each other.

I stare up at the stars and, out of the corner of my eye, catch a shooting star. I remember sitting on the boat with everyone three days ago and watching the meteor shower. My biggest worry at that time was about the text messages and who sent them. Now there's so much more to worry about. If only I had known what lay ahead.

I try to shrug the feeling of self-doubt off but it refuses to leave, hanging over me and gnawing at my insides.

I miss the gentle rock of *Newt* on the water.

I miss Mum. And I can't help but feel like this is all my fault.

The sorceress roared. She closed her eyes and her lips
parted and Gwyon knew she was casting a spell.

Gwyon turned and ran out of the cave and
into the forest. She sought out the oldest tree,
a giant yew tree. The yew gifted her one of its
branches and she made a staff out of the wood.
She coated it in bronze and carved on it the most
important spell, the gift of speaking to nature.

Chapter Twenty-Seven

Volcano

I wake, stiff and shivering, with Willow anxiously licking my hand. I don't remember falling asleep. The others are curled up next to me, eyes closed. The fire has gone out.

It's too cold for us to be out here.

The ground is damp and freezing.

'What time is it?' asks Keaton, stretching and wrapping his arms around his body.

'I don't know,' I say, looking around.

Stars streak across the sky above us.

'I feel like I could sleep for days,' says Keaton, rubbing his shoulder. 'Should we wake them?' He looks to Bryn, Aria and Enzo.

I nod, lean over and gently shake them.

'Time to wake up,' I say.

'No,' says Aria, hiding her face with her arm.

Bryn and Enzo sit up. I pass them the water bottle.

'We're pretty much at the top,' I say. 'Then it's all downhill, straight to Dad.'

Aria yawns. 'I don't want to.'

'I know. It's not much further.'

'You keep saying that,' she replies.

'Have some water,' I say, passing her the bottle. 'It will help wake you up.'

She takes it grumpily and sits up.

After a few minutes, everyone's ready to keep walking. I lead us upwards with the torch, careful to shine it behind me at times so that everyone can see.

We climb higher and my body warms up again the more I move. We walk in silence through the darkness for what feels like hours, all anxious to reach Dad.

Aria bends and picks up a stone. 'I think I found a fossil,' she says.

I shine the torch on it for her.

'Look, it has lines in it,' she says. 'I wonder who used to live up here.'

'That fossil could be from the Ice Age,' I say. 'Dad told me that this mountain was once covered by an Ice Age glacier.'

Aria smiles and slips the stone into her pocket.

As we continue to climb, the sky gets lighter. At first the east is a blue-grey and then the sky explodes into a halo of oranges, pinks and purples as the sun peeks above the horizon. Birdsong fills the air.

We reach the top and cut across the wild moorland. The landscape is covered in huge standing stones that remind me of Stonehenge.

Enzo runs ahead and climbs on top of the giant boulders, gripping with his fingers and adeptly climbing up them.

He points to the north.

I follow his line of sight and see jagged mountain shapes in the distance – Snowdonia.

The landscape changes colours as the sun hits it.

A red kite soars overhead.

We reach the summit and I spot a herd of wild Welsh mountain ponies among the moorland. A beautiful white one turns and looks in our direction. I hold my hand out and it steps forward towards me, almost close enough to touch. It has a grey dappled coat and brilliant-white mane and tail. Welsh ponies are Mum's favourite animals. I feel calm around the pony and want it to stay with us.

Seeing it fills me with hope and my jaw is set with a new sense of purpose; we've finally reached the top, and from up here it's an easy walk, straight down to Dad's cabin.

'Be careful,' says Keaton, from behind me. 'It could kick you. Don't stand too close to its hind legs.'

I roll my eyes.

'Willow. Heel,' says Enzo. She sits next to him looking up at him, tail wagging back and forth.

A stallion with strong quarters watches us from the distance. He's a chestnut with a dark mane and a white star right in the middle of his forehead. He's alert, his ears pointing towards us.

Then something startles them and they gallop off together. They jump over boulders and ravines with their manes and tails flowing in the wind. Then they disappear into the mist, as if they were never there in the first place.

The fog comes in thick and fast. It swirls and blows towards us, bringing a damp coldness. The views are gone. Suddenly we can't see anything around us except greyish-white.

'Are we in a cloud?' asks Bryn.

'Maybe,' I reply. I can only see about ten feet in front of me.

'I'm cold,' says Aria. 'I don't want to keep going.'

'Here,' says Keaton. 'Hop back on and I'll give you a piggyback the rest of the way. We're almost there, right?'

I lie my compass flat on my palm and line up the needle with north. 'East is that way,' I say, pointing into the fog. I bite my lip. 'I think.'

'I'm sure you're right,' Keaton says encouragingly. 'You're good at this outside stuff. I wish I knew as much as you about boats and plants and navigating.'

I turn and smile at him. He's just being nice

— this journey has not exactly gone to plan — but it makes me feel good inside all the same.

Maybe Keaton's not so bad after all.

December 16th – Present Day

I could never have guessed what was going to happen next. Looking back, I can think of all the things that I would have done differently if I'd known, all those breaks I wouldn't have let us take, all the items I would have packed. But at the time, I had no idea.

Gwyon hurried straight back to her home, to save her brother before it was too late. The wisdom from the potion had revealed the last ingredient Gwyon needed: three walnuts. There was just one week left before the year was over.

The sorceress chased her, getting in her way, stopping her at every turn. She cast spell upon spell at Gwyon, turning her into a snail, a rabbit and an earwig.

But now Gwyon possessed the power to turn herself back, and each time she did, the sorceress got more and more angry.

Chapter Twenty-Eight
Water

I focus on the ground in front of my feet and try to keep putting one foot in front of the other. The terrain is the same for a while: broken rock and grass. There are no trees up here.

We reach a patch of scrub where the grass isn't growing. Dotted amongst the ground lie twisted pieces of metal.

'What is it?' asks Enzo, squatting.

'There's a plaque,' says Bryn, pointing. 'Look!' He dashes over to it.

Keaton kneels beside him and reads. 'It says there was a plane crash here on the fourteenth of September in 1944. Six people died. It has their names, see? Three people survived but were injured.' Bryn looks at the bits of metal. 'And those are the remains from the plane.'

'Why did they crash?' asks Bryn.

'Maybe they hit fog,' I say. I can see how easy it would be. 'Imagine if their controls failed and they couldn't see and didn't know that they were heading straight into the top of the mountain . . .'

'That's awful!' says Aria, tracing her fingers over the plaque.

I wonder if the weather was just like this when the plane crashed. My survival book says that if you crash in a plane, you should stay with the wreckage for as long as possible, as you have more

chance of being found. I think of the survivors
– were they found here or did they venture out
into the fog?

I never thought it would be so easy to get lost
up here. The one time I came here with Dad it
was sunny, with big blue skies and views that
stretched for miles. Now I feel like we could
search these moorlands for days, looking for a
way out, unable to see anything around us apart
from the greyness. I don't say it aloud, but I can't
help shivering.

'Let's keep going,' I say, although I feel as if
I'm leading us into nowhere.

'I'm tired,' says Bryn, swinging the safe back
and forth in his hand. Enzo takes it from him
and turns the dial, trying different combinations
as we walk.

'Can I have a go?' asks Aria, after a while,
reaching for the safe.

She stops walking to turn the dial and I nudge
her onwards.

'I'm so thirsty,' she says. 'Can I have some
water?'

I dig the water bottle out from backpack but I
can tell from its weight that it's empty.

'What are we going to do now?' asks Enzo.

'Get there quickly,' I reply.

'Humans can't survive for long without water,'
says Keaton, his voice rising.

'*Three weeks without food, three days without water, three minutes without air,*' I say, repeating the words from the survival book.

Keaton takes a deep breath in.

'We're going to find Dad today, don't worry,' I say, but I'm not certain I really believe it any more. Even if we do make it to the cabin, there's a chance he's got the messages from the hospital by now and left again.

'We're children,' says Bryn. 'Do you think that means that we can survive for more or less time without water?'

'I'm sure it's longer,' I say, although really, I have no idea. I'm just trying to make him feel better.

'I'm tired,' says Aria, sitting down.

'Aria!' says Bryn. 'You keep leaving the safe on the ground. It's your turn to carry it. You've haven't even been walking for most of this.' Bryn passes the safe to her.

'I don't want to carry it any more,' says Aria. She kicks it back at him.

'I'll carry it,' says Keaton, picking it up.

Bryn snatches it from his hands. 'Actually, *I* want to carry it.'

As he takes the safe it slips from his hands and tumbles down the hill, rolling into the distance. It smashes against rocks.

We rush after it.

The safe lies against a rock which is jutting out of the side of the hill.

'That must have opened it,' says Bryn, bursting with excitement.

He reaches it first and lifts the safe up into the air. I see the disappointment on his face. It's not open. Bryn shakes his head.

'It's just chipped,' he says and lets the safe drop to the ground.

Aria shakes her head, deflated. 'I really thought that fall would open it.'

'We've been walking for hours. Do you know where we're going?' asks Keaton.

'I'm sorry,' I say. 'I really didn't think it would take this long.'

Aria opens her mouth and runs around sticking her tongue into the air.

'What are you doing?' I ask.

'I'm trying to eat the fog,' she says.

'There's a tiny bit of food left,' I say, trying to keep morale up. 'Let's sit and eat.'

We sit down, leaning against a collection of giant boulders that rest on each other.

'Listen, I think I can hear running water,' says Keaton, lifting his head into the air. He frowns. 'I've read about exposure sending you mad. Do you think I'm going mad?'

'Hush,' I say. 'I hear it too.'

Willow whines and paws at the rocks. I crawl under

one of the giant boulders and peer down. 'Pass me the torch,' I say, holding my arm back. The sunlight doesn't reach the deep corners in the shadows.

'Here,' says Bryn.

I switch it on and shine the beam of light around. 'I can definitely hear it,' I say. 'A trickle of water. It's coming from below.' There's a deep hole between two of the rocks and it stretches down and down like a well. I see the trickle of water coming through the hole.

'There's water here!' I shout.

'Is it safe to drink?' asks Keaton.

I crawl back out to examine my survival book.

How to find drinking water.
1. **Find a spring. Spring water is water that comes from the ground. It is usually safe to drink because the earth filters it and there's less chance of it being polluted. Never drink stagnant water. The water must be flowing.**
2. **Look in valleys for streams. Again, look for flowing water.**
3. **Follow grazing animals. They're usually never far away from water.**
4. **Boil any water for at least one minute to purify it.**
5. **Be wary of any water that looks polluted, has bones in it or smells strange.**

'We don't have a way to boil the water,' says Keaton, reading over my shoulder.

'I think this is a spring,' I say. 'We can risk drinking it without boiling it. But how do we get to it?'

'What do we have with us?' asks Enzo.

'I have rope,' I say, emptying the backpack.

'Do we have a cup?' asks Aria.

'No, but we do have the water bottle.' I tie the rope around the top of the water bottle with a round turn and two half hitches, the knot I use for tying the boat to mooring posts. I crawl back under the rocks on my stomach, hold the torch between my teeth and drop the water bottle down. Enzo climbs under the rocks with me and peers into the depths, trying to see the water.

I continue to lower the rope down carefully until the bottle reaches the bottom. I hold it against the current to collect the water, before slowly pulling the rope back up. The bottle gets caught on a rock and I accidently tug it too hard.

If I lose this water bottle, then that's it. Our only way of getting water, gone.

Luckily the water bottle stays attached. I manage to untangle the rope and pull the water bottle back up.

I taste it first. The water is cold and refreshing. It tastes a little bit like the earth, or how I'd imagine rocks to taste — but other than that, fine.

I let Bryn and Aria drink, and then Enzo, who then pours some out into my cupped hands for Willow to lap up. She slurps up every bit.

Keaton eyes us warily.

'Here,' I say, passing it to him. 'It's fine, really.'

He takes a tiny sip and waits, before gulping the rest down.

Then I lower the bottle back down and get another bottle full.

After four refills we're thirst-quenched. I fill it again and put it in my rucksack for later.

'I drank so much I feel sick,' says Bryn.

'Well, at least we should be good for a while,' I say, praying that this water will keep us all going for the final stretch to Dad's.

The sorceress knew the only way to catch Gwyon was to make the same potion for herself so that she had all the knowledge in the universe too. And she had to make it quickly. She didn't have three months to wait around stirring it.

Chapter Twenty-Nine
Mist

We walk with a renewed sense of energy after the spring water.

'I know we're not that far away,' I say optimistically. 'Maybe an hour tops.'

Although the mist has me feeling disorientated.

'You said that an hour ago,' says Bryn, rolling his eyes.

'And the hour before that,' says Enzo, smiling at Bryn.

'But then we can eat pasta and ice cream,' says Aria.

'Do you think your Dad has eggs?' asks Keaton. 'I'd love some scrambled eggs right now.'

If only the fog would lift.

'Where's Enzo?' I ask, whipping my head around.

'Up here!' he calls, from the top of an enormous rock. 'I thought I might be able to see more.'

'Can you?' I ask.

'Not really.'

'I'll take a look,' says Keaton. 'I'm taller than you.'

'You're not scared of the height?' I ask.

'I've been scared of everything we've done since I left my house' he says, grinning. 'What's one more thing at this point?'

He begins to clamber up, and grasps the top of the rock but then slips. He falls and lands awkwardly on his ankle.

'Ahh!' he yells, clutching his leg.

Enzo slides off the side of the rock and bends down next to him.

I run up to them both, kneeling. I unlace Keaton's shoe and pull down his sock. Willow licks his ankle.

'I don't think that's helping, Willow,' I whisper.

'Does it look broken?' Keaton asks.

His ankle looks normal to me. It's not swollen or bleeding. I reach into the backpack and pull out the first-aid kit and the survival book. I flip through the pages to the first-aid section.

Like the book says to do, I examine both his ankles next to each other. One looks a bit puffier than the other but not swollen enough to be broken.

'Well?' asks Keaton. 'Is the bone sticking out?'

'No, nothing like that. I think you're going to be just fine,' I say.

'But it really hurts,' replies Keaton. 'And if you break a leg without immediate medical attention, nerve damage can result in amputation.'

'That's *definitely* not going to happen,' I say.

'How do you know?'

'Because my book says that you don't have any of the symptoms that suggest urgent care is needed.'

'I might do.'

'Are you conscious?' I ask.

'Yes.'

'Are you suffering from blood loss?'

He lifts his head and looks at his foot. 'I see blood!'

'That's just a scratch,' I say. 'It's already stopped bleeding.'

'Oh,' he says.

'I think it's a sprain,' I add.

'How do you know all of this?'

'Mum's a nurse and I'm reading what this book says.'

Next I read how to treat a sprain.

Remember R.I.C.E

Rest.

Ice the injury for fifteen minutes at a time.

Compression. Use a bandage to stop the swelling.

Elevation. Keep the ankle elevated.

I scrunch up my face, thinking. The problem is, we can't do many of those things. We need to keep going.

How is he going to walk?

I don't think any of us can carry him.

I turn to Aria, Enzo and Bryn. 'We need something to make crutches. Have a look for two big sticks. Stay where you can see us though, and take Willow.'

'Is it me or is it getting colder?' says Keaton, wrapping his arms around himself.

'I think it's because we stopped moving,' I say, but an icy chill creeps up my spine. I bite my lip.

It was hard enough when Keaton had the use of both legs.

Now it's going to be impossible.

In the first-aid kit I find a compression bandage and slide it over his ankle, before putting his socks and shoes back on.

'Can you put any weight on it?' I ask, helping him up.

'Let me try,' he says. He puts his foot down and yelps. 'Ouch, it really does hurt,' he says. 'Why does everything go wrong every single time I try to help?'

Together we hop to a boulder, where he sits down.

I smile sympathetically.

'Mum's right,' he says, annoyed. 'Everything's dangerous.'

'We found some sticks!' Bryn and Aria appear out of the fog, followed by Enzo.

I put all my weight on the sticks; they hold and don't break.

'I think these will work,' I say, handing them over to Keaton. 'Can you walk if you lean on them?'

And at that moment, as if we need something else to go wrong, it starts snowing.

For the sorceress to create a potion as powerful as the one before in less time, she had to use whole trees and plants as ingredients. She chopped them down and lifted them into a gigantic pot, as big as a lake. But as many as she chopped, it was never enough. She kept chopping and chopping. Without the trees, soon the rivers ran dry and the animals started to die.

Chapter Thirty

Milestone

'Snow!' says Aria. She spins around and opens her mouth, letting the flakes land on her tongue.

They tumble from the sky in a blanket of whiteness.

'Isn't it a bit early for snow?' I ask, alarmed.

'Now that I think about it, Mum said something about a polar vortex reaching us,' says Keaton.

I sigh. 'It might have been helpful to know that before.'

'I didn't know we were going to be climbing mountains,' he says.

'We've got to get off this mountain before it settles,' says Enzo.

'I agree,' I say. 'Let's go.'

'But we need to be really careful,' says Keaton. 'It's already slippery.'

I set the compass again and we head east, although I don't know the exact location of the cabin, just the general direction. It's flat for ages and then, finally, we begin to head downhill. The snow continues to fall, thick and fast. It's slow going with Keaton hobbling next to us on the sticks.

Above us the lightness in the sky dims. Wispy grey clouds hang low ahead of us; behind us stretches charcoal darkness, chasing after us like the kidnapper did. The wind roars, whipping up my hair and blowing it in my face. I have no idea what time it is. As the storm gets closer, we're wrapped up in swirling thick snow and fog. I switch on the torch.

Then, up ahead, I spot some fencing at the edge of a field. I hurry; we must be getting closer to the road again. But as I get nearer, I see it's a hedgerow covered in blue netting.

Disappointed, I turn back to the others.

'Let's keep going,' I say.

'Wait!' says Aria. 'There's a bird stuck in the netting.'

I look where Aria is pointing. Behind the blue mesh I see feathers and a wing. I lift the netting gently and the bird drops to the ground, stiff and lifeless. It's all black with an orange beak.

'I'm sorry, Aria,' I say. 'It's dead.'

'Why?' she asks, pressing her lips together.

'It probably couldn't get out,' adds Keaton softly.

Aria turns without a word and rips up the netting with both hands. We all help, and soon all the hedgerow is free. Aria bundles the netting up and carries it under her arm.

'Why would anyone do this?' asks Enzo. I can barely make out his movements through the thick snow.

'I think it stops the birds from being able to nest in spring,' says Keaton. 'That way, if they need to remove the hedges, there aren't any birds in the way. I saw a tree covered in netting once and my dad told me about it.'

'It looks recent,' I add. 'Maybe they're planning

on building a road through here.'

Aria glares angrily at the netting.

'Can we bury the bird?' asks Bryn.

'Why don't we make a twig nest around it?' I suggest, quickly gathering some small twigs. We don't have any time to spare. Luckily, Bryn seems satisfied with this. We lay the bird to rest, then I pick a splinter from my thumb and lead us onwards.

We trek through the snow for about another thirty minutes, walking through fields until I finally see a change in the landscape. I stop. Ahead of us are six gigantic stones sticking out of the ground and across three of them balances a seventh, forming a huge roof.

The light is dimming around us. It's really getting dark now.

'Let's shelter under there for a bit,' I say.

We walk around the boulders until we find somewhere flat and dry. Part of the ground is covered in soft moss and the rest is coated in tufts of grass.

'This looks good,' I say. 'What do you think?' I ask Keaton.

He nods.

'I wish we could make a proper den,' says

Bryn, crossing his arms and shivering.

'I know it's not ideal,' I reply. 'But I'm too cold and tired to go looking for den supplies. At least it's somewhere to shelter for now.'

Keaton laughs. 'I've always wanted to go glamping.' He smiles me as he says it and I know he's half joking, or at least trying to make light of our terrible situation.

I smile back at him, glad he's with us right now. I catch Enzo watching us with a bemused look on his face.

We huddle underneath the stones.

I notice that Keaton is leaning heavily on his sticks and his face is pale. I think he's really in pain.

'I don't know if we can keep going,' I say, quietly. 'It's slippery and cold and Keaton's hurt.'

'Let's rest here for a few hours and see if it stops snowing,' says Enzo.

I nod. 'That sounds like a plan. We'd better make a fire.'

I leave Enzo with Keaton and Willow, and with the last of my energy collect kindling and firewood. There's not much of it around but I find a few big sticks and some loose twigs from hedges. It's already wet from the snow.

Back at the boulders, Aria leans against a stone and uses the bundled-up netting as a pillow.

I have a sudden idea.

'Can I have a look at that netting?' I ask.

She nods and hands it to me. I find the edge of it.

'Can you hold this here?' I ask her, passing her the edge. I unravel the rest of the netting and wrap it around the outside of the stones. It wraps completely around about eight times, each time forming a thicker barrier between the outside and our shelter. We have a boulder for a ceiling, three giant stones for walls, and thick netting for windows. I tie the ends together to fasten it in place and crawl underneath to join everyone, proud of my work.

'Now we have a den!' says Aria.

'It's perfect!' says Keaton.

Bryn and Enzo nod in agreement.

'I bet these rocks used to be giants,' says Aria. 'Like at Stonehenge where they all were singing together and then they got frozen mid-song by a sorceress.'

'That is so not true,' says Bryn.

'Yes, it is,' says Aria.

'Are there wild animals here?' Keaton asks, as I get back, wrapping his arms around himself and looking through the trees. 'Should we keep watch?'

'I don't think there are any that will hurt us,' I say. 'But we can take it in turns if that makes you feel better.'

'I'm hungry and cold,' says Aria, sticking

out her bottom lip and shrugging her shoulders.

We unroll the sleeping bags.

I put the kindling and the newspaper in a pile. Lighting a match, I hold it up to the corner of the paper. It catches and the paper curls.

'Please light,' I whisper.

It almost catches and I feed the last of the newspaper to the fire, but it fades and dies.

I rip out a page from the back of my survival book and light that, and the kindling crackles and catches fire.

'Yes,' I mutter under my breath.

I feed the fire the twigs, then sticks, and soon it's roaring.

We all hold our hands over the flames, warming them.

'We should take it in turns to keep the fire going tonight,' I say.

Everyone mumbles agreement.

I empty my bag and we dine on the last of the bread dipped in jam that tastes faintly of smoke.

'I wish we were all on *Newt* right now,' I say.

'Me too,' says Bryn.

'Me three,' says Aria.

Keaton nods and gazes into the fire. I wonder if he's thinking about his mum.

'What's it like to live on a boat?' asks Keaton.

'It's very hands on,' I say. 'There's always something exciting happening.'

'Once someone untied all the mooring pins and we woke up floating down the canal, bumping into other boats that had been untied too. That was kind of scary,' says Aria. 'But this is scarier,' she adds after a minute.

'How did you all end up living on a boat?' Keaton asks.

I shrug. 'Mum lived on one for a few years at university and said she always wanted to do it again. She has a thing for the waterways and only being accessible by bicycle. Mum says she loves being self-sufficient. And to be able to get up and go, if she wants to.'

'What's it like to not have any brothers or sisters?' asks Bryn.

'I bet you never have to wait to use the bathroom,' says Aria.

'Or have to share the last chocolate bar,' says Bryn.

'And you probably get lots of presents,' says Aria.

'Well, those things are true, except the presents.' He watches the fire. 'But actually I did have a sister once. Charlotte. She died when she was a toddler.'

There's a shocked silence. 'I'm sorry,' I say at last. Silky ash gathers over the fire embers. I stop myself from imagining what I'd do if something happened to one of my siblings. It's too much to think about right now.

'How did she die?' asks Bryn.

'She fell in a swimming pool.'

'What did you mean earlier?' I ask. 'When you said your mum was right about everything being dangerous.'

'Ever since Charlotte died, Mum's been scared that every little thing is dangerous. I thought she was wrong. I wanted to try new things. But now I'm not too sure. Look where I've ended up. Maybe she's right and I *should* be scared of everything.'

I shake my head.

'Sometimes scary things happen no matter what you do to stop them.'

I think of the plank and Mum slipping into the water.

'Mum says whenever I feel scared I should imagine a golden globe of light around me like a protective shield,' says Aria.

'Are you imagining that now?' I ask.

'I'm imagining one around all of us,' she replies.

'I know my mum's probably at home right now, terrified that something's happened to me,' says Keaton sadly.

Aria reaches and squeezes his hand. 'We'll all be back soon, right, Cara?'

I nod and smile, covering the uncertainty inside.

We eat our bread and jam and then we stare into the dancing flames.

I try and stay awake until I hear the gentle snoring of the twins and Enzo. I've given Enzo the torch to hold on to. The wind whistles and whispers through the trees above us and my mind turns to Mum.

'Are you awake?' I ask Keaton, who's lying next to me.

'Yeah,' he replies.

'I have a secret,' I say, gulping down the lump in the back of my throat.

He turns on to his side to face me.

'What is it?' he asks. 'I won't tell anyone.'

'It's bad,' I say. 'I did something really bad.'

'Well, sometimes saying things out loud sets those things free, so you're not carrying the weight of them all by yourself.'

I take a deep breath and say the words.

'It was my job to salt the plank the night Mum slipped on it and hurt her head. I didn't do it.'

I pause, waiting for him to say something but he doesn't.

'It's my fault she slipped. If I'd remembered to do my job, then none of this would have ever happened.'

'That's not true,' says Keaton gently. 'She could have tripped over her own feet for all you know. You're not responsible for this.'

Tears stream down my cheeks and I'm grateful it's dark.

After a while he asks, 'Can I hold your hand?'

'Yes,' I say and reach towards him.

He clasps my hand in his. 'Everything's going to be all right,' he says. 'We'll find our way home. We'll be back in school, moaning about lessons like nothing's happened.'

At that, my mind circles back to the text message. School seems so far away right now, like a different world. And, instead of feeling sad about that nasty text, now a fire burns through me, hot and angry.

How dare that person make me doubt myself?

They're the one who's hiding like a coward. Who won't use their name.

'There's something else, isn't there?' Keaton says softly.

I take a breath and tell Keaton about the message too.

'I thought you might have been the one who sent it,' I finish.

'I'd never do something like that,' he says.

'I know that now,' I say.

I drift off holding Keaton's hand. I wake up to torchlight in my face. Enzo is standing up. I think I see him look at our clasped hands and I withdraw mine from Keaton's.

'Is everything all right?' I ask, shielding my eyes from the light.

'Just going to pee,' he says.

'Stay close,' I say. I wait until he comes back and lie down before I shut my eyes again. My body is freezing. The ground is damp and I can't get warm enough. I wish I could snuggle Willow but Aria and Bryn are curled up next to her. I reach for Keaton instead and drift off with his arm around my shoulders.

December 16th – Present Day

Then, just when we thought things couldn't get any worse, they did. The storm blew the polar vortex right over us and the snow fell and fell, all night long.

Gwyon knew that she couldn't let the sorceress finish making another powerful potion; there would be no stopping her then. Gwyon realised she would have to defeat the sorceress before she could reach her brother.

And Gwyon knew that as long as there were the ingredients in the forest, the sorceress would keep on using them until they were all gone.

But Gwyon had a plan.

Chapter Thirty-One
Yew

I wake up at dawn, shivering on the ground. The fog has lifted but the snow's still falling. The landscape has been transformed into a white wilderness. Even the stones we're sheltering under have new white hats, overhanging their edges. The fire smoulders and I hold my fingers as close to it as possible to warm them up.

'Wake up,' I say to the others. I gently shake Enzo. He opens his eyes and frowns at me. Willow licks his nose. 'Everyone all right?'

They wake and stretch, stiff and tired.

Enzo's eyes widen at the snow everywhere. He shimmies out of the sleeping bag. I notice his trousers are torn and ripped from climbing.

There are new shapes and shadows all around us.

'Wow!' says Bryn, looking around. His breath comes out in thick puffs. 'Look, I'm a dragon!'

Aria joins him too. Her curls are wild and matted and her bright eyes water from the cold and wind.

I dig in my backpack for food. With the last of the bread gone, we dip our fingers into the jam and peanut butter like lollipops. Afterwards I wipe my sticky fingers in the snow.

'I never want to eat peanut butter again,' says Bryn, licking his fingers. His cheeks are red from windburn and his skin dry and flaky. For a second I think he has mud around his mouth but then I realise it's peanut butter.

'I'm sick of it too,' says Keaton. 'It's really the only thing we've eaten in over two days.'

In the daylight, now that the fog has cleared, I can see a church spire in the distance. We've descended from Carningli Mountain but we must be off course because of the fog. The church is where I thought the forest and Dad's cabin would be.

Relief floods my body. Maybe someone will be there who can take us to Dad.

'We can warm up in that church,' I say excitedly.

'Can I eat snow?' asks Aria. 'I'm thirsty.'

I consult the survival book, unsure.

Don't eat snow — it can cause dehydration. If it's melted first and purified then it's safe to drink.

I shake my head. 'I can try and melt some though.' I pack the metal water bottle with snow and place it near the embers to warm it. 'I have no idea if this will work,'

'Where are my sticks?' asks Keaton, flexing his foot.

'I may have accidentally burnt them in the night,' says Bryn. 'It got really cold.'

Keaton shrugs. 'Don't worry, I'll find some more. We would have frozen without that fire.'

'Can you help me look for new sticks?' I ask Enzo, but he busies himself packing away the jars.

I wonder what's wrong for a second but then am distracted by Bryn throwing a snowball at me.

'I'm too cold to play,' I say to him.

I check the water bottle and the snow inside is slushy. I shake it and the last of the snow melts. There's less water than I expected there to be. I pass it to Aria then repeat the process until we've all had some.

I help Keaton search and after we find a tall stick for him to lean on, we set off in the direction of the church.

'There had better be something amazing in here,' says Bryn, picking up the safe and lugging it in his hand.

I smile at him, impressed he's carried it so far.

Soon we reach the road. Tall hedgerows line it either side. There are prints in the snow from animals and birds but none from people. It's quiet and eerie. I stop before I step out on to the road. The snow covering it is smooth and clean.

Aria takes my hand. 'Explorers,' she says, smiling and looking up at me.

'Explorers,' I say. The snow crunches and compacts under my feet. It feels almost other-worldly; we are the first people to be on the road since it started snowing. I hardly want to disturb it. It looks so pretty and untouched.

I slip and regain my balance; the road hasn't

been salted. No wonder there are no cars around.

The snow doesn't stay untouched for long. Bryn storms through it, throwing powdery bunches of it into the air.

'Don't get too wet and cold,' I say, but I know it's useless. Bryn won't listen to me. Aria lets go of my hand and joins him making snow angels. The snow sticks to their hair, which I notice is filthy. As mine must be too, I expect.

Mum usually brushes theirs every day.

'Where is everyone?' asks Bryn, pointing at the desolate roads and houses in the distance.

'Probably still asleep,' I say, sheltering my eyes from the brightness bouncing off every surface.

Enzo walks off ahead of us all. I jog and catch up to him. The golden sun casts our shadows in front of us, down the hill. They're twisted and warped, showing us with extra-long legs.

'Is everything OK?' I ask. 'You seem upset.'

He shrugs.

'What is it? You can tell me anything.'

He stops on the path. He signs quickly. 'You don't seem worried about Mum. You only seem to care about holding hands with Keaton.'

Blood rushes to my cheeks.

'That's not true,' I say. 'I care about Mum getting better more than anything.'

'Then how can you laugh and joke and have

fun with stupid Keaton when she's in hospital?'

'Because I know that she's going to be OK. It never even crossed my mind that she won't be.'

I stroke his tangled hair. Big tears form in the corners of his eyes.

'Can you promise she'll be OK?'

'Yes,' I say, looking him in the eye so he knows I really mean it. 'I promise you. Mum is going to be fine.'

He nods and sniffs.

I squeeze my fists tight and hope with everything I have that I'm right.

We pass a stone house on the right. I can hardly let myself believe that we've made it out of the wilderness. Just beyond it is the church and behind the church is a hill covered in forest.

'Finally!' says Keaton, and he hobbles over to the front door and knocks.

I stand next to him and ring the doorbell.

There's still no answer.

'It's light so it must be seven thirty or eight by now,' says Keaton. 'Surely someone's awake.'

'It's Saturday,' I say. 'Maybe they went away for the weekend.'

'Maybe,' replies Keaton, staring up at the windows.

I shrug and lead us onwards, disappointed. Even with buildings around it still feels like we're in the middle of nowhere.

We approach the church. The grounds are enclosed by a stone wall. I push the gate and enter the graveyard. The path to the church is lined by ancient yew trees and gravestones dusted with snow. It's dark and shadowy. I glance at the dates written on the stones as I pass.

I've always liked looking at the names on gravestones, seeing if there's anyone related to each other, or looking for my name. I've found *Cara* twice but have never found an *Enzo*. I've found *Bryn* several times, especially when visiting Dad.

'Look, there's Arianwen,' I say, and we gather around.

'I wonder who she was,' says Aria.

'She lived for eighty-seven years. That's really old,' says Bryn.

A huge gust of wind rustles the flat needles of the trees. Willow howls, long and sorrowful. It's so loud it makes me jump and I knock into a tree. Snow falls on to my neck and shoulders.

The wind seems to twist the branches, so that they reach down for us, as though they've come alive. I grip the trunk to steady myself. I touch something wet and sticky. My hand comes away dark red.

I scream, and run towards the church entrance.

Gwyon used her staff to call all the trees to life. The oaks stretched and yawned and prepared for battle. The hazel bushes shook and roared at the sorceress. The downy birch trees safely hid their woodpeckers and nesting birds and raised their elegant drooping branches, ready to fight.

Chapter Thirty-Two
Safe

'What is it?' asks Enzo as he catches up to me.

'Are you all right?' asks Aria.

'Cara? Are you OK?' asks Keaton.

I stand flat against the stone wall of the covered entrance and breathe heavily.

What was that?

I look down at my hands streaked with thick red.

'You're hurt!' says Bryn.

Enzo bends and sniffs my hands.

I pull them away. 'What are you doing?'

'It smells like sap,' says Enzo. 'It's not blood.' He heads back towards the trees.

'It's OK,' says Keaton. 'You're OK.'

But I know that something is wrong. I just don't want to say it out loud. It felt like there was something else in the graveyard with us. Something that I couldn't see. I could feel it prickling up my spine and in the adrenaline racing around my body.

Enzo reappears and beckons us back to the trees.

I follow him reluctantly.

'It's a bleeding yew tree,' he says and points to a sign on its trunk.

'Do all yews bleed?' asks Keaton, confused.

Enzo shakes his head.

I walk around the trunks of the trees next to it. Bryn clutches the safe in his arms and follows me. Aria grabs on to his hand, not wanting to be left alone in the graveyard.

The other yews have honey-coloured sap dripping from their fluted trunks, but on the one I touched red sap drips over the flaky bark.

I wipe my hands off on the snow. It leaves a red mark.

'Let's go inside and see if anyone can help us,' I say, trying to shake off the feeling I had. 'Come on.'

Under a stone archway, I push the heavy wooden door. It clicks and opens.

'Hello?' I shout. 'Anyone here?'

My own voice sounds like a ghost echoing back.

Light streams in lines through the stained-glass windows.

I walk around.

'Look for a map of the area,' I say. 'Churches sometimes have maps for visitors.'

Keaton flicks through the leaflets by the entrance.

By the back window, a Celtic cross made of intertwined lines is etched along the stone window frame. It looks like the shape of a person lying down.

Underneath the opposite window frame, on the stone wall, there are vertical and slanted marks etched in a horizontal line. I feel drawn to them and step closer. Below the markings is a plaque explaining that it's the ogham alphabet and next to it is a sign with a key to decoding it. Each grouping of lines, or etches, corresponds to a letter in the alphabet. It was used around sixteen hundred years ago to inscribe messages, names or writings on stones.

I've seen markings like this before. I rub my fingers over them.

They're like the lines on the safe.

My heart thumps loudly. Maybe those markings on the safe aren't just scratches. Maybe, just maybe, they're a code.

'Look!' I shout, beckoning at everyone. I explain to them about the alphabet. Bryn brings the safe around and positions it so that we can see both the sign on the wall with the alphabet key and the etched lines on the safe.

'See,' I say, pointing at the markings. 'These four slanted scratches make the letter "F", right?'

'Then that one is an "O". And a "U".'

'And "R",' says Enzo.

'Four,' I say. 'It must be the first number of the lock code.' Excitement builds in my stomach.

I meet eyes with Enzo and smile.

'We're going to find the treasure,' sings Bryn and he does a dance around the safe.

'What's next?' asks Aria.

'N-I-N-E,' I say.

'Then T-E-N,' says Enzo.

'T-O,' I say. 'It must be two. There's no symbol for the letter W.'

'O-N-E!' Keaton says. 'We did it.'

Bryn carefully turns the dials to match the numbers. 'This is it!' he says, and he pulls the door.

It stays stuck.

'Come on!' he yells, and yanks harder.

'Let me try,' I say, taking the safe from him. I say the numbers aloud as I spin the dial, concentrating. '4, 9, 1, 0, 2, 1.'

This time there is a loud click. Bryn stares up at us, mouth dropping open with excitement.

'Here,' I say, passing him the safe. 'You do the honours.'

Bryn prises the stiff door open and reaches in.

I grin at Keaton, Aria and Enzo, almost not believing that, after all this time, we're going to find out what's inside the safe.

Bryn pulls out a broken wooden stick. He tosses it aside and pokes his head in.

'Where's the treasure?' he asks. 'It's empty!'

Aria picks up the stick and examines it.

'You've got to be kidding me,' says Bryn, shaking his head at the stick. 'I carried that safe everywhere for a stick!'

'We should have thrown it back on the canal when we found it,' says Aria.

'But why would that kidnapper want a stick?' asks Keaton thoughtfully.

I think for a second.

'He must have the wrong safe,' I reply. 'The one he's looking for is probably at the bottom of the canal still.'

Keaton laughs. 'It's pretty funny.'

'It's *not* funny,' says Bryn.

'It's a little bit funny,' says Keaton. 'You have to admit that.'

Bryn gives a small, reluctant smile.

'I guess we're not bringing a million pounds to Mum any time soon,' I say.

'What would you buy if you had that much money?' asks Keaton.

'First, I'd repair *Newt*, then I'd buy my own really nice narrowboat,' I say.

'You wouldn't want to live in an actual house?' asks Keaton.

I think about it. I think about the nasty text message and how maybe Dad left because he didn't want to live on a houseboat.

I glance around at everyone: Bryn chewing his top lip in annoyance about the safe; Aria twirling the stick around; Enzo laughing at Bryn; Willow happily curled up on a stretch of rug; even Keaton, who's searching for a map, and I feel proud of them all. I'd do anything to be back on *Newt* with them and Mum right now, no matter what anyone else thinks about it.

'Well?' asks Keaton, glancing up, and I realise I never replied.

'I'd miss the water too much,' I say. 'And cycling along the towpath, summer cruises down the canal and waking up to ducks outside my window. Don't get me wrong, it's not all fun. I forget every year about how cold it gets if the wood-burner goes out, and sometimes there's ice on the inside of the windows. But I can't imagine living anywhere else.'

And it's true, I realise. I wouldn't trade it for anything in the world.

It was the oak trees who found the sorceress.
They lifted her up into the air, wrapping
her arms with their branches.

A holly plant pricked her thumb and
let the magic power drain away.

Gwyon stood and watched, holding her staff.

'Do it,' said the sorceress. 'Kill me now.'

Gwyon shook her head. She didn't want to
kill anyone. She left the sorceress to live in
a cave, with no power left in her, forced to
forage for food, with only bats for friends.

Chapter Thirty-Three

Rainforest

'I found a map!' says Keaton. 'Is this where your dad lives?'

He points to a place labelled 'Pengelli Forest Nature Reserve.' It's right next to the 'You Are Here' arrow.

'That's it!' I say, picking up my backpack and standing. 'That's where Dad is!'

'Then we really are close,' says Keaton. 'Apparently it's just next to us.'

We step outside the church and I use the compass to determine which direction to go in. With a map to line it up to, now I can make sure we're going the right way. Aria carries the stick tucked under her arm. As we leave the graveyard the yew trees rustle and the wind whistles through the branches.

We walk along a footpath behind the church, through the forest on the hill.

I chew my lip. I'm worried it's taken us so long to get here that Dad won't be there. But if that's the case he'll surely know that we could be heading to his cabin. If we're not at *Newt*, at the hospital, or at Keaton's then he must realise that this is where we'll be. There isn't anywhere else we know to go to.

After a few minutes, we pass the ruins of an old farm outbuilding. Vines and tree bark have twisted their way through the bricks. It seems no one lives in this area. It makes me feel miles and miles from people. We peer in through the glass windows. New shoots push through the cracks, engulfing the walls in roots and vines. They grow sideways and in unusual shapes. Inside, a tree has pushed its way through the floor and the trunk has grown straight towards the back window and out the other side.

'I bet there are lots of spiders in there,' says Aria.

'I would love to have a tree growing in the middle of my home,' says Enzo.

I glance up at the trees, turning slowly. Above us are gnarly moss-dripping oaks and an ash and birch canopy. It's the understory of hazel trees, the shrub layer, that tells me that we've arrived in the Celtic rainforest, along with the boulders smothered in moss. They're covered in snow but I can still see the bobbly shapes of the moss underneath.

My favourite time to visit is in May when all the trees have bright new green leaves on them and underneath is a sea of purple bluebells and a bright-green carpet of moss.

'I didn't know we had rainforests in Britain,' says Keaton from ahead.

'It's a temperate rainforest. Dad says some of the woodland plants, like hazel, have been growing in this area since the end of the last ice age. The landscape has stayed the same.'

'What does that mean?' asks Aria.

'She means you don't have to imagine what it *used* to be like, because this *is* what it was like,' says Enzo.

'I wonder if anyone lived here?' asks Aria.

'I don't know,' I say. 'You'll have to ask the rocks and trees. They're the only ones who have seen it all.'

'And the sorcerers, witches, fairies, giants and dragons,' says Aria.

We walk through a grove of trees, which bend to form an archway, white and dripping in icicles, into a wintry world.

I brush against a fern and snow tumbles off, revealing unfurling green stems. I remember Dad teaching me a word for being surrounded by lots of ferns. *Rhedynog*. I whisper it under my breath.

'I think there's a stream down there,' says Bryn, running ahead. 'I can hear it!'

I hope so — we've gone a while without water. We walk on a blanket of moss. Strange-shaped lichen, lungworts and liverworts cling to trees, dotted in patches of snow. A red robin flits and flies along ahead of us.

'I feel like I'm on another planet,' says Keaton.

I stare up around us and smile. Finally, after everything, we've arrived.

We step into a gorge and there's a waterfall up ahead, with a river running from it.

I drop the backpack and dash and kneel by it. I fill the water bottle and let Bryn and Aria drink, then cup my hands and drink myself, scooping water into my mouth. Even Keaton goes straight for the water, too thirsty and tired to care about if it's clean. I look up and a frog stares back at me from on top of a rock.

Soon we'll see Dad.

And then we'll get to see Mum again.

I wonder if she's awake.

I imagine her worrying about us and being told about *Newt*, abandoned and burgled.

I hope I haven't made anything worse by leading us here.

'I'm tired of sleeping outside,' Aria says suddenly.

'We won't have to tonight,' I say and this time I'm sure. I actually remember this place. 'Dad's cabin is just up there.'

I lean up against a tree to tie my shoelace. There's a hole in the trunk at eye level.

Some fur in the hole catches my eye. Curled up in a nest of honeysuckle bark is a dormouse, fast asleep, snuggled against its own fluffy tail. Luckily it's sheltered by the wood from the snow.

I put my finger to my lips and beckon the others to look.

'Is it dead?' asks Bryn.

'No,' I say. 'Asleep.'

'Can I hold it?' asks Aria.

I shake my head. 'It's hibernating for winter, safely tucked away from everything. We can't disturb it.'

'Can I just stroke it?' she asks hopefully.

I shake my head and smile. 'Just look, that's all. We're really lucky to see one.'

There's a tap on my back and I spin around. Bryn stares up at me with watery eyes. His mouth is wide open and he sticks out his tongue. It's bright purple. He tries to scrape the purple layer off his tongue with his fingernails.

'It's yucky,' he says.

'What did you eat?' I ask, furrowing my brow. 'Here, rinse your mouth out.' I pass him the water bottle.

'A berry,' he says, spitting purple on to the ground.

'You're not supposed to pick berries you don't know,' says Aria in a matter-of-fact tone.

'I thought it was an edible one that Mum picks. I'm so hungry,' says Bryn.

I run through a list of all the poisonous berries in my mind. Holly berries. Yew berries. Mistletoe berries. Most of them are red coloured, not purple.

'What colour was it? What did it look like?'

'It was black.'

My stomach tightens. Deadly nightshade has black berries. They're extremely poisonous.

'Where did you find it? Can you show me?' I ask, trying to keep my voice calm and steady.

He nods and points to a bush with spikes. I sigh with relief. It's a blackthorn bush.

'It was just a sloe berry that you ate,' I say to Bryn. 'You'll be completely fine.' I ate one raw once. The sharp taste dried my whole mouth out in an instant, but it wasn't harmful.

He nods, his purple-stained lip jutting out. I can tell he's exhausted and there are deep circles under his eyes.

Above us, nimbostratus clouds hang dark and low in the sky. They appeared quickly, blocking out the sun. I frown at them and I shiver as the air gets even colder. Keaton has found more sticks to lean on but I can tell his limp is getting worse.

Finally, up ahead I spot a path lined by stones and at the end of it, a wooden cabin. 'There's Dad's cabin!'

'Dad!' shouts Bryn, running forwards. He trips over a stick and falls. 'I'm OK,' he says.

But he's cut his leg on something. Blood streaks down from his knee, through his trousers.

I open my backpack, grab the first-aid kit, and press a bandage against the gash to stop the bleeding. Then I stick the biggest plaster we have over it and scoop him up into my arms.

I just have to get us all ten steps further.

Then all of this will be worth it.

Dad will fix everything.

Gwyon was finally able to go to her brother. She rushed back to her family home, where she had left him just over a year ago. But when she got there, she was too late. The sorceress had kept her captive for too long. Her brother had died.

Chapter Thirty-Four
Lichen

Aria runs up to the door and rattles it.

'Dad?' she shouts. She bangs her fists against the wood.

There's no answer.

My stomach drops.

He has to be here.

'There,' I say, spotting a rock balanced on the front step. Even on *Newt*, Dad would leave a key under a rock.

Aria lifts it and there's a key underneath. She slides the key into the lock and opens the door.

'Dad?' I call, stepping inside. I adjust Bryn in my arms.

Dad's not here.

'Maybe he's coming back in a minute,' says Aria, optimistically.

My heart sinks. After everything we've been through, I really thought that Dad would be here, waiting for us.

Outside, the snow starts to fall again, thick and fast.

I lie Bryn down on the sofa and open Dad's wood-burner, piling logs on the fire. My fingers are numb and I fumble with the matches. Luckily the wood is dry and catches quickly, crackling and popping.

'Everyone come and warm up,' I say. 'We have to stay here and wait for Dad to get back.' Even if

Dad isn't here, we've made it to shelter. And that's something.

Keaton hobbles over to the kitchen and opens the cupboards, finding baked beans. He empties them into a saucepan on the stove to cook. Our drawings decorate Dad's fridge, pictures of dragons and unicorns and funghi.

I grab towels from a cupboard and hand them out, using mine to dry the ice-cold droplets from my hair. Papers are strewn across the table, covered in numbers and diagrams of lichen.

I search around for a phone. But I know that Dad doesn't have a landline.

My fingers ache as the warmth comes back to them.

'Breakfast, lunch and dinner is served,' says Keaton.

Enzo and Aria leap forward to help carry the food.

'I'm ravenous!' says Aria.

The warm beans are comforting. We all gather around the woodstove. Bryn is huddled on the sofa.

'We may as well burn this stupid stick too,' says Bryn, tossing it towards the fire.

I pick it up. The light of the flames through the glass door illuminate patterns on the side of the stick. 'Wait,' I say. 'There's something written on it.'

We examine it; on the side are drawings and engravings. I don't know what they mean.

'Maybe it is something special after all,' I say.

Bryn grins and clasps it in his hand.

'Look what I found,' says Aria, pulling out a box from under the coffee table. 'Old photos.'

We sift through them. There's pictures of all of us on *Newt* together, before Dad left.

Keaton falls asleep sitting in a chair and gently snores.

'What was it like when he lived with us?' asks Aria.

I forget they were only three when they got divorced.

'When you were babies sometimes he would hold both of you, one in each arm. And Dad was always the one who would give us chocolate biscuits and sweets.'

Aria smiles and sifts through the photographs.

I rest my head on a cushion and look at them over her shoulder. Then I drift off, exhausted and full of warm food.

Enzo shakes me awake, worry in his eyes.

'What is it?' I ask.

I follow his line of sight. Bryn's skin is warm and sweaty. I look at his knee and see the scratch from earlier has swollen. It must be infected. I'm annoyed at myself. I didn't clean it properly.

I grab the first-aid kit, wake Bryn up and take him through to the bathroom, where I run his leg under the tap in the bath. I spot a tiny piece of gravelly-looking stuff stuck in the wound. I find tweezers by the sink and a lighter, which I use to sterilise them.

'This will hurt a little bit,' I say.

Bryn cries out as I pick out the bit of gravel. Aria strokes his head and Enzo holds his hand.

'It's all out,' I say.

I squeeze some antiseptic cream from my first-aid kit on to the cut. Then I put on another dressing.

I hope Dad gets back soon.

I already feel responsible for Mum being in hospital.

I can't let anything happen to Bryn too.

I lean my head against the window and watch the snow tumble outside.

Aria has found Dad's snack drawer and munches happily on chocolate and muesli bars.

Outside, the snow is piling up higher and higher.

Soon we'll be stuck inside here.

I check on Bryn, sleeping soundly on Dad's bed. I place my hand on his forehead. It's hot and clammy.

'I need to go and get help,' I say.

I open Dad's cupboards and pull out all of his warm clothes: jumpers, waterproof trousers, gloves and a hat.

'What are you doing?' asks Keaton, waking up. 'You can't go out there.'

'I'm worried about Bryn,' I say, lowering my voice so Aria can't hear. 'The cut is clearly infected. And if I wait much longer we'll be stuck in here.'

'We'll come with you,' says Aria, walking over.

'No,' I reply. 'You stay together. There's only enough warm clothes for one person. Bryn's hurt. Keaton's hurt. I know where I'm going. I'll be fine.'

'I don't like this,' says Keaton. 'I don't like this one bit.'

'Take Willow,' says Enzo.

'It's too cold for her,' I say. 'And look how tired she is.'

Willow lies on her stomach, legs stretched ahead of her, fast asleep in front of the fire. Her ears prick up at the sound of her name, but she keeps her eyes firmly shut.

I repack the backpack with food and water and an extra torch.

Aria searches the cupboards and finds Dad's badminton rackets — it's his favourite game. We used to set up a net in the fields together and play every summer.

'I can make you snowshoes!' With Enzo's help, she saws off the handles with Dad's bread knife and ties my shoes to the rackets with string. 'It should make walking a bit easier,' she says.

'Thanks,' I say, glancing at Bryn. His skin is grey and ashen. He looks dangerously ill.

Outside the snow piles up under the windowsill. Soon there'll be no way to get out.

I take a deep breath. *I have to go now.*

I wave goodbye and heave the door open against the weight of the snow.

'I'll see you all soon!' I say, and, ignoring the worried expressions staring back at me, I step out into the arctic chill of the blizzard.

In her grief over her brother, Gwyon felt the push and pull of the potion inside of her, trying to take advantage of her vulnerability, trying to control her.

Gwyon wanted the power out of her; she could sense how dangerous it was. So she transferred the power to her staff, pouring all of the magic out of her body and into the wood. That way the power was at Gwyon's fingertips but not inside of her. She had control of it but it couldn't control her.

Chapter Thirty-Five
Alone

I venture out wearing my homemade snow shoes. My feet are heavy. Bundled up under so many layers with the big shoes I must look like a space person, attempting to walk on the moon. My mission: to get to the nearest house and find help.

Crocuses push up through the snow, reminding me of Mum. I bite my freezing lips. I can't cry now; the tears might freeze my eyes shut.

Something catches my eye and I pause. A hedgehog lies in a ball in the snow in front of me. I know that hedgehogs shouldn't be out in the daytime. It means that there's something wrong. I stare at it closely, a tiny bundle of needles. On closer inspection, I see the spines are brown, black and white tipped.

I don't think it's a baby hedgehog, a hoglet — or, as Aria calls them, 'hedgehoglets'. I lean over it.

'Hi there, little one. Are you all right?'

I scoop it up with my gloves and hold it under my jacket, trying to warm it up.

'Why aren't you hibernating?' I ask. After a minute it relaxes its spines and unravels from its ball. I let out a sigh of relief. It's alive. I peek under my jacket and see its cute pointy nose and dark eyes.

'It's just you and me out here. We've got to go and find help,' I whisper to it. 'Then I can get you some help too.'

The landscape changes as I keep walking. From Dad's, I remember the direction of town. There are more conifer pines and rhododendron trees. I know they're non-native, invasive species.

I'm leaving the ancient woods behind.

Once I'm out from under the trees, the landscape turns to fields filled with mushrooms half hidden under the snow.

Everything around me looks alien, covered in big snow drifts. It's eerie and quiet.

Where is everyone?

I try to calm my imagination and focus on the snowflakes falling and tumbling from the sky. I find it soothing to spot one and try and follow it as it falls.

A wind picks up and I have to squint to protect my eyes.

There's a rustle behind me and I immediately think of the kidnapper. I glance over my shoulder. There's no one there.

I have to remind myself that we don't have wild bears. It must have been a fox or a badger. Quickening my pace, I hurry over the snow. My heart races.

The cold cuts through my clothes, making my bones ache. I ignore it and press on. I climb over a stile and land awkwardly on the side of my snowshoe and it snaps loudly, breaking in half. Losing my balance, I plummet face first into the snow, tucking my hands to my chest to try and protect the hedgehog. I roll over, sit up and spit out a mouthful of cold snow. I check on the hedgehog. It sniffs me and stares up at me with wide big eyes, cosy in my armpit.

'That was close,' I whisper to it.

Without the snowshoe, I'm in trouble. It's going to be nearly impossible to walk now.

I rub my eyes. They're dry and grainy, as if they have sand in them.

It's so cold and so white that it feels like the end of the world.

Should I turn back?

I can't. I'm their only hope, their only chance of getting everyone out and saved. I shiver uncontrollably. Now that I've stopped moving, the heat is draining from my body.

I hear rustling again and whip my head around. I can't see anything through the blizzard. I drag myself crawling forward on my hands and knees, trying to get away from the noise.

I freeze.

A stag, appearing from nowhere, stops in front me. It has red fur and huge velvety antlers with snow dripping from them.

Behind him stand more deer. They stop and look at me.

I stay still and watch them. Everywhere is silence except for the ringing in my ears and the blood pumping through my body.

After a few minutes they trot onwards, disappearing into the blizzard.

The stag leaves me invigorated and able to think more clearly.

Freezing air hurts in every breath. I dig in the backpack for my survival book.

'It might have tips to keep warm,' I say aloud.

Exposure to the cold is dangerous and could result in hypothermia.

I check my hands. My skin is already red, numb and tingly.

I flick through the pages to see what I have to do.

Seek shelter.

I close my eyes and the brightness of the snow all around leaves a glowing red light on my eyelids.

I have to keep going.

If I stop I'll catch hypothermia.

I bite back tears. I wonder how everything could have gone so wrong so quickly. From all of us on the roof of *Newt*, to Mum alone in the hospital, to me alone in the snow.

When Mum and Dad got divorced she said that sometimes things happen that we can't control. I take a deep breath and open my eyes. The blizzard rages around me.

I stand and my thighs and muscles burn. My broken snowshoe sinks deep into the snow. I yank it out and try again, skating forwards on it instead of taking steps.

There's something in the distance. A building, I think. It's hard to tell with everything being white and blurring into each other.

I force myself to plough onwards and the building disappears out of sight again. I squint and see rainbows. I wonder if I'm hallucinating. I sink back down in the snow, deflated. There's nothing I can do; pain rips through every part of my body. My skin is cold but also burns at the same time. I must have even imagined the building.

Too many things have gone wrong now. Even if I could fix the snowshoe, my feet and legs ache too much to move. I don't even know where I'm going. There's nothing around us except snow.

I open my coat and glance at the hedgehog.

'I'm sorry,' I say to it. 'I tried. I really did.' My voice breaks. I clutch at my arms and rock forward, tears streaming down my cheeks.

December 16th – Present Day

When I think back to that moment, I really believed that I was going to freeze in the snow. My whole body had given up.

And then I remembered something that my mum said to me about running marathons.

Today I can do this, one step at a time. *A camino largo, pass corto.*

She called it her mantra and she repeats it any time the going gets tough or when she thinks that she can't possibly run another step.

Gwyon buried her brother in a burial mound on top of the highest mountain, the old volcano.

Unbeknownst to her, ever since she defeated the sorceress and saved the forest, people had been watching her. Gwyon had drawn attention to herself. And as she was saying goodbye to her brother, someone crept up and stole her staff.

Chapter Thirty-Six

Hedgehog

I remember Mum's words and repeat them in my head. I push myself up, out of the snow, until I'm standing.

'One step at a time,' I say, but I'm in agony as I move forward. Everything hurts. I wish I was covered in protective spikes like the hedgehog. I imagine that I am and picture them shielding me from the coldness of the snow, like armour.

'Today I can do this,' I say, my voice a bit stronger now. As I make it up the slope, the building reappears; it had just disappeared out of sight, hidden by the hills.

'Yes,' I say, more powerful with every step. I don't look up but at my feet and focus on moving them forward. 'One step at a time,' I mutter again and again until I'm close enough to see that the building is a farmhouse. The windows are lit up and smoke curls from the chimney.

'We're going to be just fine, hedgehog,' I whisper, stroking its smooth spines with my gloved fingers.

I walk slowly, being careful not to fall again, worried about squashing the hedgehog. My breath comes out in puffs of condensation. I haven't seen this much snow ever.

A Border collie sits in the window and barks as I get closer.

I ring the doorbell, over and over again.

'Hang on, hang on. I'm coming,' calls a voice.

An elderly lady opens the door, looks me up and down.

'Get in here quickly, dear,' she says.

'Thank you,' I say. I try to explain but it takes all my energy just to follow her inside.

'Sit here by the fire,' she says. 'My name is Lowri.' She fetches blankets and drapes them over my shoulders.

My body shivers and shakes.

She returns a few minutes later carrying a tray with a steaming teapot and chocolate biscuits. She pours me a cup and I clutch it in my hands, warming them up.

And then I'm able to talk and I tell her everything.

As soon as I finish blurting everything out, she says, 'That's the most exciting thing I've heard since one of our sheep had triplets. I bet there's lots of worried people out there looking for you and I know you're concerned about your brother, but I think the first thing to do is try calling your dad.'

'And an ambulance for Bryn,' I say.

'My neighbour's a doctor. She's retired now but I'll see if she can go and check on your brother. It'll probably be quicker than trying to get an ambulance in this snow.'

She brings me a phone handset, plus more food, bananas and a bag of crisps. 'I don't have much food in the pantry right now, dear. Here's the phone.'

'Thank you,' I say, feeling the hedgehog move under my jacket.

'Just one more minute,' I whisper to it.

'I'll be back in a tick,' says Lowri.

I ring Dad's mobile. It's the only number I know off by heart. If he doesn't answer I'll have to call the police.

'Hello?' It's Dad's voice on the other line.

'Dad!'

'Cara? Is that you?'

'It's me,' I say, hearing the relief in his voice.

'Where are you? I'm at the hospital with your Mum.'

'I'm near your cabin. We came here but you weren't there.' My voice cracks.

'What? How did you get there? Are you OK? Are the others with you? Are—'

'We're all here,' I say, interrupting him. 'Dad, Bryn cut his leg and I'm worried he's sick. The lady, Lowri's, gone to get a doctor.'

There's a silence on his end as he takes in my words. 'Don't go anywhere. I'm coming to get you.'

Lowri returns and I ask her address and tell him.

'Can I speak to her?' asks Dad. I pass him over.

She listens for a moment and then says, 'That's no problem. She can wait with me. Drive carefully. The roads are very bad out here.'

'The doctor's heading to the cabin now,' says Lowri, after we've said goodbye to Dad.

'Thank you,' I say. 'Do you have any cat food?' I add.

'Why on earth would you want cat food, dear?'

I open my jacket and show her the little hedgehog. 'I rescued it on the way here. I think it got too cold.'

'I have just the thing,' she says and goes off.

She returns with a hot-water bottle for the hedgehog and puts it in the corner of a cardboard box under blankets. We offer the hedgehog some cat food and she twitches her little nose and laps a few bites up.

'That's a good sign,' she says. 'A very good sign.'

I sit and whisper to the little hedgehog, stroking her from head to back. Her spines are smooth to touch and her underbelly is fluffy. I never imagined a prickly hedgehog being cuddly but this one likes to climb on to my lap and curl up in my jumper. She looks up at me with her big eyes. I realise I didn't get a chance to ask Dad how Mum is on the phone.

I'm sure she's all right.

But the familiar sinking in the pit of my stomach is back.

It takes Dad three hours to drive from the hospital to the farmhouse. As soon as I hear the hum of his engine outside, I fling the door open and rush out into the cold, bundled up in all his clothes. I wrap my arms around Dad.

'I was so worried about you, bug,' he says, holding me close. Even though I haven't seen him in a while, he smells the same, of leather and pine. I bury my face on his chest.

'I'm here now,' he says, stroking my hair. 'Everything's going to be OK. I'm not going anywhere.'

I wrestle my head away and meet his eyes. They glisten. I don't even have to ask him. He looks at me and says, 'Mum's all right. She's still sleeping but they think she's going to be just fine. Don't worry.'

And I sob quietly into his coat.

After a while he says, 'Come on. Let's go and rescue the others.'

I wipe my nose with my sleeve and nod.

'Your son is going to be OK,' says Lowri. 'The doctor is with him now.'

We thank Lowri. 'Do you want to leave the hedgehog here?' she asks. 'I'll let her out in the garden when she's better and you can come and visit.'

I don't want to leave the hedgehog. But I don't have any way to care for it. I pick it up and cradle it in my arms. 'I'll come and visit you,' I whisper to it. 'And you're going to get really strong so that next winter you're big enough to hibernate. Bye, little one.'

Gwyon searched for the staff for years and years. She travelled north to the great lakes and to the flat levels in the south. But she couldn't find the staff anywhere.

After fifty years, she decided to set up her own home back in her beloved forest, surrounded by her favourite trees. She taught other people the healing potions she'd learnt when she gained all of the wisdom of the world.

Chapter Thirty-Seven
Legend

Dad parks his van at the top entrance to the Celtic rainforest, only a few minutes away from the cabin. I can't believe that my epic journey through the snow to the farmhouse has only taken ten minutes in a car.

We climb out and hurry through the forest to his cabin.

'I always thought you lived really far away,' I say to Dad. 'But we found the cabin in a few days . . . and we were on foot.' I stop, unsure of how to say what I want to next. 'Why don't you try harder to see us more often?' I pause again, remembering the text message, thinking that maybe he never wanted to be on the boat with us at all. 'Is it something I did?'

He stops and kneels in front of me, shaking his head. 'Of course not.' His voice breaks. 'You're perfect. I love you just the way you are. Don't you ever forget that, OK?'

I smile and nod.

'I know I haven't done a good job of keeping in touch recently,' he continues as we walk. 'I'm so sorry if I made you feel that it was your fault. I get so wrapped up in my work. But I think about you all the time.'

'You do?'

He nods. 'I can't wait to show you what I've been working on and hear about your new school.'

'I'd like that too,' I say, smiling.

I spot movement and see a stoat, all white with a black-tipped tail leaping in arches over the snow. We stop and watch it disappear into the whiteness, Dad's arm over my shoulder.

We reach the cabin and the snow has got so thick that the doctor had to dig a tunnel through to reach the door. Dad throws the door open.

'You found him!' says Aria, and runs towards us.

Enzo's right behind her, throwing his arms around Dad.

'This is our friend Keaton,' I say.

Keaton waves.

'I've spent the past few days with your parents,' says Dad to Keaton. 'They've been very worried about you.'

Bryn lies on the sofa with his leg elevated over the arm of the chair. 'You made it!' he says, reaching up to hug Dad.

A woman with long grey hair wearing a sheep's-wool jacket holds her hand out to Dad and introduces herself. 'I'm Maisie. I've been watching him closely and his temperature is back down. Better take him to be checked out though.'

Dad nods and takes her hand. 'I can't thank you enough.'

She glances at her watch. 'I'd better be getting back myself.' Maisie smiles and says goodbye to everyone before heading out.

Dad feels Bryn's forehead and looks at his knee. 'It's looking good,' he says. 'And no fever. That's a very good sign.'

Dad spends the next hour fussing over us and cooking pasta and sauce and finding us clean, dry clothes.

Once we're all fed, clean and dry, I ask, 'Can we go and see Mum now?'

'I need to see my parents too,' says Keaton.

'Of course,' replies Dad. 'They're waiting for you.'

Dad lifts Bryn up and carries him in his arms. Keaton leans on me and hobbles through the snow path Dad carved out. Enzo and Aria walk alongside us.

Once we're in the van and driving we listen to how Dad arrived at Keaton's house the night we disappeared and how he searched everywhere with the police and Keaton's parents for us. They found my shoes outside the shelter, then they found *Newt* next to the city. They used sniffer dogs to track our scent but it disappeared at the train station.

'That's when I got really worried,' he says.

We fill Dad in on our story.

'I'm so proud of you,' says Dad. 'I'm so proud of all of you.'

I notice some of his eyebrow hairs have turned grey. He's usually clean shaven but stubble covers his chin. He looks older than I remember.

There's a lull in the conversation as we drive through a town I don't recognise. Children are having a snowball fight in the street.

'All the schools were closed on Thursday and Friday because of the snow,' says Dad. 'It might not even clear before Monday.'

'Are you going to tell the school about the text messages?' asks Keaton, whispering to me.

I shrug. 'I don't know. After everything that's happened over the last few days, they don't seem as important now.'

Besides, I think to myself, I don't feel self-conscious about the boat any more. It's my home and that's all that matters.

'I would like to find out who sent them though.'

I wonder if any more messages came through to my phone while we were away.

'You said just three people from school knew your number?' he asks.

'As far as I know.'

'I think I can do some digging,' he says.

'What about you?' I ask. 'Are you going to talk to your mum about letting you leave the house without worrying so much?'

He smiles. 'Definitely. Although I might not tell her about some of this adventure.'

I laugh.

'Where are we going to stay?' asks Aria as we get closer to home.

'With me in the hotel until we can get the boat up and running again,' says Dad.

'What's going to happen to Willow?' asks Aria, concerned. Willow wags her tail from the back of the van in response to hearing her name. It bangs against the seat.

'I'll look after her while you visit your mum in hospital,' says Keaton.

'She can't go back to that shelter,' Bryn says.

'I know,' says Keaton. 'And don't worry about Mum. It's time we made some changes, and having Willow to stay can be one of them.'

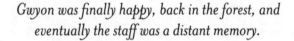

*Gwyon was finally happy, back in the forest, and
eventually the staff was a distant memory.*

*But the yew tree never forgot. Until
the staff was returned, it would bleed,
for a part of it had been stolen.*

Chapter Thirty-Eight
Blood

We reach the hospital after a few hours and the doctors check on Bryn's and Keaton's legs. Keaton's mum and dad meet us there too.

It's already early evening and dark outside.

Keaton's ankle is sprained but not broken. Before he leaves, he stops beside me.

'I'll see you at school?' he asks.

I nod. 'Depending how Mum is, I might come next week.'

'Sounds good,' he says, and he waves as he leaves.

I smile after him. I know that school's going to be different from now on, in a good way. I finally have my friend.

While the doctors are talking to Dad about Bryn and how to keep his leg clean, I sneak out, and stand outside Mum's room. I take a deep breath and push the door open.

It's only been a few days since we've seen her, but it feels like for ever. My hands are shaking. She's still asleep, still in the induced coma. My heart sinks.

After everything, I thought she'd be awake by now.

I hold her hands; they're warm.

Fear comes flooding back. I'm more scared than ever that she'll never wake up.

I undo my backpack and find the picture of us all, her teddy and her lucky quartz. I place them on her bedside table. It's the only thing I think to do to help.

The police meet us out in the corridor and Bryn reluctantly hands over the stick to them. We tell them about the kidnapper and everything that followed.

'We're doing everything we can and we'll provide protection but you have to be vigilant, and let us know of anything out of the ordinary,' says the police officer. 'We haven't found the kidnapper. He's still out there.'

The next day, back at Dad's hotel, we sit on the tidy beds and scroll through the channels. After three nights of sleeping outside, I expected to love being in a comfy bed, but all I can do is worry about Mum.

I sigh and hug a pillow. There's nothing worse than waiting. The clock on the wall slowly ticks along.

After another day and night in the hotel, we've all had enough.

'Where are we going to live?' asks Aria.

'Are we going to have to stay here in the hotel for ever?' asks Bryn.

Dad shakes his head. 'You'll be back on *Newt* in no time.'

'But she's still covered in smoke,' I say.

'And the window's smashed,' says Enzo.

'Then let's go and fix it,' says Dad, standing up. 'No point us all moping around here.'

Outside, the snow has melted into sludge, and we all go to *Newt*, along with a police escort. The boat looks sad and lonely all by herself. The snow has transformed the towpath into a new slippery mud world.

'First things first,' says Dad. 'I'll fix the window, and you guys can start by getting rid of that smoke smell.' He opens the cupboards and pulls out a bottle of vinegar. 'We had a fire in my house as a child, and this is what my dad used. Grab a sponge each and wipe the walls with it.'

'Now it just smells of vinegar,' says Bryn, pinching his nose as he starts in the living room. 'I'm not sure which is worse.'

After a while the smell makes me gag and I step outside for some fresh air. Lying across the back of the deck is the plank, the one that Mum slipped on.

I grab the plank and throw it into the water. It dips under for a moment, then floats on the surface and bangs against *Newt*'s hull. Ducks swim towards it, quacking, thinking there's food alongside it. I want the plank to crack in two and smash.

I should have salted the plank. It was one stupid tiny mistake.

If only I could go back in time and change it.

On the way back to the hotel, Dad drives us past our schools.

'I think you all need something to keep your mind off everything,' he says. 'The teachers have set some work aside. Run in and get yours, Cara.'

As I round the corner, I spot Keaton in the yard and smile. I make to walk over to him.

Then I freeze.

He's leaning against the wall of the main building, talking to Jasmine.

I duck behind the wall. I edge as close as I can and hear him talking.

'I hated the boat,' he says. 'I don't know how anyone could ever live on there.'

I feel my skin burn.

I think about everything we've been through together out in the wilderness: how I cared for his sprained ankle; shared my biggest secrets with him; the time he comforted me and held my hand. I thought we were really friends.

How can he say those things?

I wait until I hear Jasmine say goodbye to Keaton and walk away, before I step out from behind the wall.

'Then I don't know you at all,' I say. He spins and I turn away, walking quickly in the other direction, fighting the stinging tears in the corners of my eyes.

I knew I couldn't trust him.

'Wait!' shouts Keaton, running after me. He catches me up but I don't stop. 'I was just saying that to find out if it was her who sent the text message.'

'I don't care,' I say.

'I promise I was just trying to help.'

'Well, don't. I don't need your help.'

'I'm sorry,' he says, his head dropping.

'I thought you were my friend,' I say.

I storm towards the gates and Dad's car. Visiting school was a mistake.

'Cara!' calls a different voice. 'I'm so happy you're here. I was about to post this.'

Ms Pepper hands me a large envelope. A card. I don't want to open it just yet. I can't trust what it'll say inside and I don't think I can handle anything else mean right now.

'Thanks,' I say.

'Are you all right? We're here if you need to talk. I know you're going through a lot.'

'I think I just need to be with my parents right now.'

I try and smile and quickly leave.

Outside the gates, once I'm alone, I stop and open the envelope and look at the card. It's filled with messages:

I can't believe you were KIDNAPPED. So happy to have you back.

Did you know that you're famous?!

I was worried to hear about everything that happened. Thinking of you.

It's *nice*. Everyone is being nice.

I turn and run back through the gates, catching up to Ms Pepper.

'Actually,' I say, slightly out of breath. 'There is something I want to tell you about.'

She leads me into her empty classroom.

I'm nervous telling her and butterflies gather in my stomach as I speak.

I've survived the wilderness, I think. *This can't be so hard.*

I spill everything about the text messages, no longer feeling ashamed.

She asks me to show them to her on my phone so she can note down the number.

'We take bullying in all its forms very seriously here,' she says. 'I want you to know that.'

'Thanks,' I say, turning to leave with a spring in my step, feeling lighter than I've felt in ages. Almost as if I'm back in the river floating.

🌿

Back at our hotel, a police officer waits outside. We go upstairs to Dad's room.

'Can I have my stick back?' asks Bryn immediately.

'That's why I'm here,' says the police officer. 'It's actually not a stick, but a rare artefact believed to be one and a half thousand years old. It was stolen from the museum in Bath five years ago.'

'What kind of artefact?' asks Aria.

'They believe it was a staff of some kind. It has writing carved into the side of it.'

'Do we get a reward?' asks Bryn, grinning.

'The museum are very happy to have it back,' replies the police officer, amused. 'So happy in fact, they'd like you to unveil the new exhibition celebrating its return.'

'I knew it was treasure!' says Bryn, and he jumps on the bed to celebrate.

The magic didn't enjoy being stuck in the staff and was always looking to be set free. It needed someone to control.

For hundreds of years, every person that owned the staff would have good luck. But over time, the person would realise the power the staff had over them. They would become frightened of the staff and its magic. But when they tried to get rid of the staff, it would leave a bit of magic behind and give them bad luck.

Chapter Thirty-Nine
Family

A few days later, it's time for the museum opening.

We drive past Keaton's house to get there. My stomach flips, nervous at the prospect of seeing him today. I notice his tidy garden and remember how I used to believe that his house looked perfect but then I think about how imperfect it actually was living there. I'd rather live with my messy family any day.

'I wish Mum could see this,' I say to Enzo.

'Me too,' he says.

The museum manager gives us a personal tour when we arrive and lets us examine the staff before anyone else gets to see it.

'You know, legend has it that the staff has magical properties. It can make nature come alive,' he says, lowering his voice.

'I wish we'd known,' says Keaton, his voice teasing. 'We could have got the trees to carry us back.'

I ignore him, still annoyed with him for talking to Jasmine.

'Now, let me show you the ribbon you'll be cutting,' says the manager.

'I'll be right there,' I say, transfixed by the staff. I know we're not supposed to touch it, now we know it's a precious artefact, but I reach forwards. After the unveiling it will be locked behind glass anyway. I rub my fingers over the engravings on the side, the spell.

'Please,' I whisper. 'If you really are magic, make Mum better.'

And as I touch it, I get the same creepy feeling I had in the graveyard, by the yew tree.

'Were you talking to that stick?' asks Keaton from behind me.

I jump and spin around.

'No.'

He raises his eyebrows at me.

'Maybe. It's private,' I say.

'I understand,' he says. He gestures to the door. 'Everyone is waiting.'

'OK,' I say and break his eye contact.

'It was Jasmine who sent the text message,' he says.

'It was?' I ask.

He nods. 'I promise I'm not lying. I said those things to get her to admit it to me.' He steps towards me. 'I was just trying to help. It worked. She told me after you visited school that day.'

Jasmine, I think. It makes a funny kind of sense that it would be her.

'I understand,' I say, softening towards him.

'I feel terrible. Can we forget about it?'

'Happily,' I say.

He opens his arms and we hug each other.

'We should get to the ribbon cutting,' I say, pulling away. 'Come on, let's go.'

As we walk down the corridor side by side my thoughts turn to Jasmine. I'm sad it was her. We've been friends since we were six. Or at least, I thought we were friends.

What did I do to her to deserve those messages?

Nothing. All I tried to do was be friends.

And in that moment, I realise that there's nothing I could have done differently to prevent it. All those things she said to me and everything she did to exclude me this term and at Bonfire Night, actually had nothing to do with me at all. It was always about her wanting to fit in at school and trying to feel better about herself by putting me down.

Outside there's a crowd and a local news team filming. Everyone smiles and cheers at us, but I can't bring myself to smile back. It all feels wrong without Mum there too.

We cut the ribbon.

Afterwards I talk to the museum curator. 'It's a beautiful artefact,' I say.

'I agree,' he says. 'Thank you for being such a wonderful guardian of it.'

'Have you ever thought about taking it home to Wales?' I ask. 'There's a church there where – where I think it would be really happy.'

The curator raises his eyebrows at me. 'I'll have a think about it,' he replies.

Out of the corner of my eye, I spot a man at

the back of the room. There's something about the way he moves that's familiar. I see his face, his beady eyes and searching expression.

A flash of green sticks out of his pocket.

It's the kidnapper.

I tap the curator on the shoulder and whisper to him. 'I think that's the man that stole it.' I nod towards the back of the room.

'I'll get the police,' the curator says immediately, and hurries off.

'Do you think it's really him?' asks Aria.

'Positive,' I say.

We watch from a distance as two officers approach. He makes a dart to the door but he's handcuffed and led away.

'Why does he want it so badly?' asks Bryn.

'I don't know,' I reply. 'I don't know if we ever will.'

Dad wakes us up early the next morning. 'Let's go, let's go,' he says. 'We need to get to the hospital.'

'Is Mum OK?' I ask, my stomach turning. 'What's happened?'

'They woke her up this morning,' he says, with a smile. 'And they're very pleased. She's getting better.'

Enzo raises his arms into the air and Bryn

runs a victory lap around him. Aria tugs at my
jumper and bounces up and down on her tiptoes,
excitedly.

'Now listen, it could still be a while before she
gets fully better. And we need to be quiet when
we visit her, all right?' says Dad.

'We'll do anything, Dad,' I say.

Outside her hospital room, Dad lets me go in
first. Mum's sitting up. Her eyes are open. She's
awake.

'Mum!' shout Aria and Bryn from behind
me, running towards her.

I forgot how beautiful her eyes are. They're a
deep brown like the trunk of an oak tree.

All four of us squeeze under her arms.

'We missed you,' I say.

'I missed you so much,' she replies. 'The only
thing I remember about being asleep is wanting
to wake up to see you.'

She strokes my hair and kisses the tops of our
heads.

'Thank you for taking care of them,' she says
to Dad, who's standing in the doorway.

'Oh, they're the ones that took care of me.'

Behind Mum's bed, on the windowsill, I
notice the crocuses have opened. Their blue

marbled petals catch the morning sunlight.

My heart bursts with happiness that we're all together.

'You'll be better before you know it,' I say to Mum.

'One step at a time,' she replies. '*A camino largo, pass corto.*'

I smile; even though Mum's in hospital and *Newt* still needs some fixing, I feel like this is going to be the best year yet.

December 16th – Present Day

We found out all about the kidnapper from the police a few weeks afterwards. He confessed everything.

Let me tell you, he wasn't your ordinary kidnapper or burglar. He believed that his family had been given good luck from the stick. It had been in his family for years. He knew all about the staff, about the ogham alphabet and the legends surrounding it.

But one day, he lost the stick and his luck changed. After that, he was desperate to get it back. So desperate that when he found out it was in a museum, he stole it and hid it away in a safe.

His luck didn't last very long. On the way home, going over a bridge, he ended up in a long line for a police check. He figured that the museum had noticed the missing relic and called the police. Panicking, he wrote the combination for the lock on the side of the safe in the ogham alphabet, just in case he forgot it. And then stepped out of his car on the bridge and pretended to be admiring the view. But really, he dropped the safe in the canal.

He came back later to search for the safe but could never find it again until years later when he saw us on the news, holding it.

And that is the story of how we found a safe that would change our lives for ever. But not for the reasons we expected.

I finish talking and close my notebook, staring out at the faces from the Christmas assembly who are all looking back at me. Their eyes are riveted. Then everyone claps and cheers.

I beam and walk to sit down in the audience. Aisha and Sophie gesture at me to sit next to them and I smile and wave but keep on walking. I pass Keaton, who gives me a thumbs-up, but again, I don't stop.

There's a seat right next to Enzo, Bryn, Aria, Mum and Dad, and that's the one I'm heading for.

The following week the staff was moved to the church. Back under the protection of the trees and the ancient forest, the magic was contained. And the yew tree was finally able to stop bleeding.

THE END

Author Note

My aunt, uncle and cousins live in Wales and every school holiday I would spend time with them there: swimming in the freezing sea, walking over the rugged cliffs, running through the ancient woodlands. The Welsh land is steeped in mythology and legend and, when I was growing up, different snippets stood out to me. In the tradition of fairy tales, I have borrowed from some of these stories and retold them in a way that feels relevant to the world we live in today.

It was only a few years ago that I discovered that the ancient woodland in Wales is in fact a temperate rainforest, also known as the Celtic rainforest. This prompted more research and a longer stay in Wales, which is where I discovered the Ogham alphabet at St Brynach's Church, the plane crash in the Preseli hills and the importance of lichen in the ancient forests at Ty Canol and Coed Felinrhyd. As always for me, it's the settings that spark the stories. Although the places in this story are real, I have taken a few poetic liberties with the route the characters travel.

A few parts of the story are inspired by my own

life: from the age of eighteen until I was twenty-three, I lived permanently on a narrowboat along the Kennet-and-Avon canal and I loved cycling along the towpath to get to work and university, watching the herons, ducks and swans, and cruising the boat on a sunny day.

A less fond memory that I drew from was being bullied in my last year of primary school. This continued into secondary school as I was cast out by a group of girls that I thought were my friends – just like Jasmine tries to exclude Cara. By the time I was thirteen things were much better but looking back, I wish I had realised some of the things Cara learns in this story a bit sooner. If you or someone you know is being bullied, tell someone you trust. Although it may feel like it, you are never alone.

Acknowledgements

To my editor, Lena McCauley, for shaping this book from conception into the best book it can be and whose clarity of vision saved me from multiple moments of anguish about plotlines and characters. I'm so grateful to have you by my side through this writing process.

To my wonderful agent Sallyanne Sweeney, it is such a joy to share this writing journey with you. Thank you!

To my family, as always. You all mean the world to me. A special thanks to my husband and partner in life, Jonathan, for being my sounding board on all book ideas and problems, your help with my research, and ongoing support.

To everyone at Hachette Children's Books, my publishing family, thank you so much for turning this story into beautiful books!

To Dom Kingston, publicist extraordinaire! I have the best time working with you!

To Rob Biddulph, for gorgeous illustrations that bring the book alive. Thank you so much.

To my aunt, Hazel Merriweather, for not only being my Welsh guide but also for reading and offering advice on an early draft. To my mum Anya, and sister Rachel, for making my research trips possible and being my adventure companions.

To my friends, especially Emma, for sharing your love of Wales and making me climb Snowdon for the first time when we were younger!

To Angelica Ramos, for all your help and ideas with the Spanish.

To Alex Davies and Louise Starkey, for feeding me inspiration in the form of ancient artefacts, chats about archeology, long walks, and cups of tea.

To the lovely community of UK children's authors, including my workshop group and friends, Jennifer Newbury, Sarah Shillam and Mel Darbon.

To all the educators, librarians, booksellers, teachers and parents, for promoting reading for pleasure. Every day I'm overjoyed and encouraged by the support from your wonderful community.

And thank you, readers! I hope you enjoy this story.

Also by

JESS BUTTERWORTH

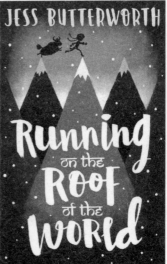